T0170585

MURDER ON THE THIRTEENTH

Also by A. E. Eddenden
A Good Year for Murder

Murder on the Thirteenth

By
A. E.
Eddenden

Academy
Chicago
Publishers

Published in 1992

Academy Chicago Publishers
213 West Institute Place
Chicago, Illinois 60610

Copyright © 1992 by A. E. Eddenden

Printed and bound in the USA by the Haddon Craftsmen
Printed on acid-free paper
No part of this book may be reproduced in any
form without the express written permission
of the publisher.

Library of Congress Cataloging-in-Publication Data

Eddenden, A. E.
        Murder on the thirteenth / A.E. Eddenden.
            p.   cm.
        ISBN 0-89733-380-2 : $18.95
        I. Title.
    PR9199.3.E32M8   1992
    813' .54–dc20   92-22964
                                              CIP

MURDER ON THE THIRTEENTH

Chapter One

On January 13, 1943, the biggest and most complete blackout in the history of North America took place. At precisely 9:00 p.m. the sirens wailed. The citizens of Fort York turned their lights out. They were joined by two and a half million other persons in Southern Ontario and areas in the states of New York, Ohio and Pennsylvania in an international wartime test. Despite inadequate alarm systems and the element of surprise, the mock air raid went off well. Most people co-operated.

After all, there was a war on. The west coast, authorities said, lived in fear of a Japanese invasion. Numerous confirmed German U-boat sightings had been made on the Atlantic side of the continent from Newfoundland to Florida.

Yet there were those lulled by the smug complacency of living as far inland as the Great Lakes who didn't take the matter seriously. Specifically, they left their lights on. Tonight they would answer to the vigilant.

Inspector Albert V. Tretheway, FYPD, appointed Regional Officer, Air Raid Precaution in Fort York for the duration, sat wedged in the passenger seat of Jake's '33 black Pontiac, straight-eight convertible.

"There's one now," Tretheway pointed.

Jake turned the car roughly, making fresh tracks in the snow-covered street toward the offending light. He braked sharply. Tretheway rolled his window down and the two glared at the unsuspecting, well-lit living room.

"Go get 'em, Jake." Tretheway said.

"Me?"

"You."

Jake grumbled under his breath but left the warmth of the car. The unshovelled snow crunched under his feet as he jumped up the verandah steps. He knocked on the frost-covered storm door and waited. Looking back, Jake could see the pulsating red glow of his boss's cigar hovering dangerously close to the cloth roof of his beloved convert-ible. Tretheway's shadowy bulk seemed to fill the whole of the car's interior.

The moon eased out from under the clouds to throw undulating shadows of evergreens and telephone poles across the snowdrifts. A whirling breeze blew snow-flakes up and around the tree trunks and bushes. One lone walker, clutching a fedora to his head, pushed his unbuckled galoshes across the quiet night scene. Most people stayed inside because of the blackout. The un-naturally darkened homes looked deserted.

The inside door opened. "Yes?" The man's muffled shout came through the glass of the storm door.

"Warden Small." Jake touched the brim of his dishpan-shaped steel helmet with his right finger. "Your light is showing."

"Eh?" the man shouted back.

The glass was beginning to fog up. Jake could make out the blurred figure of a middle-aged man in his undershirt cupping his hand around his ear. The man opened the door. Heat poured from the foyer. The sound of ABC Radio's "Gang Busters" clashed with the cold outside air. A dog barked.

"Your light's on," Jake shouted.

"I know," the man said. "It's night time."

"Who is it, Harvey?" A woman's voice called from inside.

"I'm sorry," Jake persisted. "I'm an Air Raid Warden." He pointed his flashlight at the large, hand-painted 'W' on the front of his helmet. "You'll have to turn your light out. It's a blackout. Didn't you hear the sirens?"

"Is it a real air raid?" the man asked.

"No," Jake explained. "It's just a practice. A pretend bombing."

"Then let's pretend I've turned the lights out." The man smiled at his own wit.

"Good one, Harvey," the woman said.

"How do you feel about a summons?"

Jake turned toward the voice. The man and woman peered around Jake. At the bottom of the verandah steps Tretheway stood, feet apart, in his police issue, size 13 boots. He shone his five cell flashlight on his front so there could be no question of identification. His oversize, navy blue greatcoat, with the gold insignia of an FYPD Senior Officer, hung open to reveal a casual, bright red sweatshirt with the official crested message, '1941 INDI-VIDUAL CHAMPION TORONTO POLICE GAMES'. The upward beam of light gave his scowling face an eerie appearance. Because of his height (6'5") and his weight (280 lbs.) his helmet looked a lot smaller than Jake's. Jake wondered where the cigar had gone.

"Or perhaps a trip downtown," Tretheway finished.

Jake turned back to the couple.

"I'll get that light." The man disappeared inside.

"When can we turn it back on?" The woman asked.

"When we're told," Tretheway said.

"There'll be an all clear siren, Ma'am," Jake had memo-rized the ARP manual. "A continuous signal at a steady pitch."

The door closed. Jake heard the dog yelp and stop barking. The light went out.

"What's the time?" Tretheway asked.

"End of 'Gang Busters'," Jake said. "Must be 10:30."

They were back in Jake's car resuming their ARP patrol in the traditionally quiet west end of the city.

"Let's get down to the office," Tretheway said.

"Right." Jake pointed the long nose of the Pontiac downtown.

In 1941, Tretheway was, in effect, lent to the war effort by the Fort York Police Department. Jake, or really, Jonathan Small, Constable 1st Class, went with Tretheway as his able driver and assistant under the same plan. As Regional Officer, Tretheway had no particular sector, but was responsible for the ARP function of the whole city. The police, fire and other emergency vehicles patrolled the industrial and commercial sections of town. They were assisted by the Royal Fort York Light Infantry (Reserve).

Tretheway and Jake shared a downtown office on the ground floor of the Fort York Arms with Geoffrey Beezul, another full-time employee ($1 a year man) of the wartime office. Beezul was old family Fort York. He was affable, bit of a name dropper, member of the right clubs, handsome in a coiffured, Nelson Eddy sort of way, but had an annoying habit of hitching his expensive, ill-fitting pants up every few moments.

Thin, wet-eyed Zoë Plunkitt, commandeered from the Genealogical section of the FY Public Library, rounded out their group as a part-time secretary. She blinked constantly. The rest of Tretheway's force, mostly Air Raid Wardens, were made up of civilian volunteers.

Jake nudged the car into a snow bank beside the "No Parking/Taxi Stand" sign at the entrance to the Fort York Arms. He stepped carefully out of the car into ruts made in the snow. Tretheway stepped into the snow bank and felt the snow trickle over the tip of his ankle-high boots. He looked at Jake. Jake shrugged an apology.

A whistle sounded. Luke Dimson strutted, as only a short person can strut, toward them. He handled the job of doorman reasonably well, but with his limited attention span, often wandered from his post. For the last few years, Luke had whistled for taxis and willingly handled cumbersome steamer trunks as easily as if they were loaves of bread. A thick shock of auburn hair pushed out from under the decorated visor of his military-style cap to almost touch his black eyebrows, which met in one furry horizontal bar. Luke's eyes were set much too close to his stubby, slightly twisted nose. His uniform was always clean, his gloves spotless and his whistle shiny but over-used; like now.

The whistle sounded again. Luke spat it out, knowing the painstakingly-whitened lanyard around his neck would stop its fall. "You can't park there," he began, then recognized Tretheway and Jake. "Hi, Jake. Didn't know it was you."

"Hi Luke," Jake said. "That's okay."

"I'll watch the car for you, Inspector." Luke touched his cap.

"Hold the whistle, Luke," Tretheway said.

"Sure thing, Inspector." Luke smiled broadly. "How's the blackout?"

"Fine, Luke," Tretheway said. "Just fine."

The lights shone brightly in the office but the blackout curtains shielded them from the street. It was a long, thin office that had been a fashionable shoe store before the war. The front door opened off the same wide sidewalk as the hotel's covered entrance. Three desks stood in a row. The first, with its vase of dried herbs, implied a receptionist or secretary. Geoffrey Beezul's came next, then Tretheway's, the biggest desk of all. On the back wall next to the rear door, Jake sat, when necessary, at a large utility table. Running along the wall opposite the desks, rows of open

5

cubicles held the tools of the ARP trade; neatly piled gas alarms, flashlights and batteries, boxes of whistles, hand bells, knapsacks, binoculars, steel helmets, gas masks and many, many information booklets. Several stirrup pumps stood in one corner. A faint, not unpleasant, odor of leather still hung in the air.

Geoffrey Beezul was standing at his desk when they arrived. His coat, helmet and flashlight lay on his desk.

"Tretheway. Jake." Beezul hitched up his pants. His alert blue eyes flashed between them. he looked younger than his forty years. "Sort of exciting out there."

"Where's Miss Plunkitt?" Tretheway looked around the office.

"I don't know," Beezul said. "Is she supposed to be in?"

"Doesn't she work here?" Tretheway asked.

"Well yes," Beezul said. "Part time."

"Maybe she's stuck in the snow," Jake suggested.

Tretheway looked at both of them. "I hope the Luftwaffe will be as understanding as you two in a real air raid."

"At least the phones aren't ringing," Jake said.

The phone rang.

For the next hour, the three of them fielded calls from the concerned citizens of Fort York. Most who reported uncovered lights on verandas or from inside houses where the blinds were not properly drawn were referred to their local block warden. One warden called to see if the raid was real. Tretheway made a note of his name. Someone called from a beer parlour. The regulars were arguing about whether that noisy gas alarm you twirled around your head signalled the start or finish of the attack.

"The start," Beezul explained patiently. "When the gas has dispersed, we ring a hand bell. Sounds much nicer."

A family requested the plans for a shelter like the one Greer Garson and Walter Pidgeon had in *Mrs. Miniver*. And there were others who just wanted to be Air Raid Wardens and share the glamour of steel helmets and stirrup pumps.

The number of phone calls dwindled. Blackout or no blackout, it was a week night and the people of Fort York were going to their beds. Only one phone call bothered Tretheway. And then just a little.

"That was an odd one." Jake hung up the receiver.

Tretheway looked a question.

"Someone reports a light on the marsh."

Tretheway blinked.

"A flickering light, she said," Jake went on . "like a flume."

"Marsh gas?" Beezul suggested.

Tretheway shook his head. "Too cold."

Beezul took a call.

"Could be a crank," Jake said.

"Or moonlight on the ice," Tretheway said.

"I've got another one." Beezul covered the mouthpiece. "Same place."

"Tell them we'll look into it," Tretheway said.

Jake raised his eyebrows.

"What's the time?" Tretheway asked.

"Quarter to twelve," Jake said.

Tretheway pulled on his large nose. "Let's go, Jake." He looked at Beezul. "It's slowing down anyway."

Beezul nodded in agreement. "Have fun on the marsh." He smiled at Jake.

Jake frowned.

Chapter Two

The drive from their downtown office to the west end took about fifteen minutes. Clouds of blowing snow didn't help, but the main roads were ploughed and, at this hour, there was little traffic.

Jake stopped the car at the top of the big hill that led to the eastern end of the marsh.

"Can't see anything from here," Jake said. "Too many trees."

"We'll have to go down," Tretheway said.

"It's pretty steep," Jake said.

Tretheway didn't answer.

"And icy."

Tretheway pointed down the hill.

Jake put the car into first and inched ahead. They started their descent, straining against the lower gears.

"What are we doing?" Tretheway asked.

"Gearing down," Jake answered.

"Why?"

"It brakes the car. With the engine."

"Don't you have real brakes?"

"This way is more efficient."

"And noisy," Tretheway concluded.

Jake bit his tongue. Tretheway, as the former Head of the Traffic Division, knew all the rules and regulations concerning vehicular legislation. He was considered a theoretical expert on traffic. But he'd never learned to drive. Jake, on the other hand, loved to drive and it showed in his natural aptitude behind the wheel of any vehicle. At the bottom of the hill, Jake pulled the car off the road into a snow drift until they were almost stuck.

"Have to walk from here, Boss," he said.

Tretheway grunted and got out of the car.

The two trudged through the pristine snow towards Princess Point. It took them five minutes. They stopped at the top of a slight embankment and stared across the frozen marsh.

In the late 1780's, Captain Thomas Coote, a British officer from Niagara, took to hunting in this area of the New World exclusively. In his account of the marsh, he said, "I have never seen such a variety of wildfowl as comes to this place." Coote had found his paradise.

The area survived early European explorers, United Empire Loyalist settlers, seventy-foot Durham sail freighters, the Desjardin Canal construction, picnickers, canoeists and bird watchers until it fell forever under the care and protection of the Fort York Royal Botanical Gardens.

Tretheway appreciated this, especially on his Sunday walks, but Jake harboured an attachment born of familiarity, for this large tract of land, marsh and open water, know as Coote's Paradise. He had run the trails as a child, kayaked and played hockey on the marsh and, except for the Ammerman thing three years ago, had pleasant memories of the sanctuary.

"Now," Tretheway said. "Where do you suppose that light is coming from?"

"If at all," Jake answered skeptically.

Their eyes swept the horizon, first to the left, past nearby Cockpit Island and Sassafras Point to University Landing and Willow Woods in the distance. Then, with the visual aid of the old pilings, black spots against the ice, they followed the Desjardin Canal to Rat Island, Bull's Point and Hickory Island.

"What's that?" Jake said.

"Where?"

"Hickory Island."

"Which one's that?"

Jake pointed straight across the marsh. Tretheway strained his eyes in the direction of Jake's finger.

"I can't see anything."

They both stared at the island. From where they stood, it appeared to be no more than a grey smudge, slightly darker and closer to them than the opposite shore. Jake shivered in the raw cold. The sky was clear for the moment, the moon full and the wind fitful.

"I saw something," Jake said.

"What was it?"

"There it is again!"

"I see it."

It disappeared. For a second, maybe two, they'd seen a light, an illumination of some sort, a flume of fire from Hickory Island, then a return to darkness.

"What was it?" Jake asked after a moment.

Tretheway shook his head. The wind picked up noticeably and blew clouds across the bright face of the moon. Behind them, the city still lay in enforced darkness.

And then the light appeared again, this time a brighter, dancing flame that lasted a full minute. Then a wild flaring, a dimming, then gone again.

"Let's go," Tretheway said.

"Right." Jake started back for the car.

"Where're you going?" Tretheway asked.

"You said..."

"This way." Tretheway started unsteadily down the embankment.

"Shouldn't we phone, or something?"

"No time."

Jake followed his boss to the marsh's edge.

Tretheway tested the ice with his boot. "Should be all right," he said.

"Been close to zero all week," Jake said.

Tretheway took three or four, then five tentative, sliding steps away from shore.

"How is it?" Jake asked.

"C'mon." Tretheway started carefully toward the island that was a good quarter mile away. Jake slithered after. The moon reappeared and lit the shimmering silver of the smooth ice that was not blanketed by snow. Walking through the snowy parts was relatively easy. It was the clear portions that gave them trouble. About halfway there on a section of glare ice, Tretheway took off. A gust of wind caught his bulk and he sped, without moving his feet, in the direction of the island. When he stretched out his arms instinctively for balance, his jumbo-sized greatcoat became a sail and his speed increased.

"Wait for me!" Jake shouted.

Tretheway sailed before the wind, across the marsh as gracefully and efficiently as the Durham boats had done one hundred years before him. He had to fall. When Jake caught up to him, Tretheway was sitting heavily in the slight depression he had made in the ice.

"Okay, Boss?" Jake asked.

"Get me up."

With much grunting and cursing, but mainly with Jake's help, Tretheway regained his feet.

"Can you see anything now?" Tretheway winced.

"I don't think so," Jake said. "Hard to tell. Shadows. Wind blowing the snow around. Did you hear anything?"

Tretheway seemed surprised. "When?"

"Before, " Jake said. "When you were making your move." Jake sensed Tretheway's disapproving look.

"What'd you hear?"

"I don't know," Jake said. "Maybe a voice."

"Probably the wind."

"Probably."

The rest of the way was snow-covered and easier footing. At the island's edge they slowed cautiously to a stop.

Hickory Island was sixty feet long and about half as wide. Only a few spindly trees misshapen by decades of winds blowing across the open water and bunches of scraggly bushes existed on the hard-packed mound of earth. At no point was its elevation higher than ten feet. Some irregularly shaped rocks made an unnatural pile in the clearing at the island's centre.

"Keep your eyes open." Tretheway took out his flashlight and started up the easy slope towards the rocks. Jake followed. Tretheway stopped suddenly and held Jake back with his outstretched arm.

"Look." Tretheway pointed his light on the ground.

"Someone's made marks in the snow," Jake said.

"And then tried to cover it up." Tretheway followed the half-obliterated line with his flashlight as best he could. It traced a large uneven shape around the pile of rocks.

"A circle?" Jake asked.

Tretheway nodded. "There's more." The light picked out several snow-scuffed areas. "Can you make anything out?"

"Numbers. One, six. Is that a nine?"

Tretheway brought the light closer. "I think so. And a two."

"What's that mean?"

"Don't know." Could be anything from a secret code to a date."

"Like 1692?"

Tretheway nodded. "Anything else?"

"Not really," Jake answered. "Just a minute. That could be a triangle."

"More like a star. Looks like they were in a hurry."

"Probably heard us coming." Jake thought about whoever had been on the island first hearing a shout, then looking up to see a 280-pound bat-like creature sailing towards them. "Or saw us." Jake smiled.

Tretheway didn't reply. He moved toward the centre of the clearing where there was enough moonlight to show that the pile of rocks had been laid to protect a wood fire.

"There's your light," Tretheway said. "Or what's left of it."

Jake bent over the still softly glowing embers. "What's that smell?"

Tretheway sniffed. "Sulphur."

"Could be from STELFY." Jake was referring to the Steel Company of Fort York in the adjacent Fort York Harbor which occasionally spewed sulphur fumes into the atmosphere.

"Maybe." Tretheway shined the flashlight on the smooth rocks at the edge of the dying fire. While Jake watched, he adroitly slipped his free hand under his armpit, squeezed off his glove, and gingerly picked up one of the rocks. "Not too hot." He examined it closely, then scraped it with his fingernail. "Wax."

"What?" Jake asked.

"Wax," Tretheway repeated. "There's your big flare-up. The wax caught fire. Must've spilled out of this." He put his glove back on and picked up a blackened metal bowl from the centre of the fire. Tretheway poked the solid contents with his mitt. "More wax."

All of a sudden, Jake felt uneasy. He looked over his shoulder, then did a complete sweep the other way. The moon disappeared again and the indecisive wind scattered the few remaining embers of the fire. A dog howled. Jake shivered again but this time not from the cold.

"You're saying someone was out here, middle of nowhere. Midnight. Freezing cold. And during a blackout. Cooking wax over an open fire." Jake paused. "Why?"

Tretheway shook his head.

"And where are they now?" Jake said.

"He , she or they, whoever it was, has to be over there." Tretheway pointed to the north shore, a scant furlong away.

Jake didn't say anything.

"What's over there?" Tretheway asked.

"A fair-sized hill. There's a path through the woods. Leads to a small parking lot. Then the highway. Follow it to Wellington Square. Or come back around Wellington Square Bay and the marsh to Fort York. To where we are, if you like."

"We should go over." Tretheway stared at the yards and yards of smooth ice separating them from the far shore. He could see no one. A conservative estimate of twenty miles an hour entered his head. That would be about the speed he'd reach before he slammed into the hill if the rising wind caught his greatcoat again. "Maybe in the morning."

"Right," Jake sighed.

Tretheway turned to go As he ducked under a branch, a shape not made by nature caught his eye. Swinging from a low limb of a stunted black willow was what looked like an untidy piece of string. He snapped on his flashlight.

"What now?" Jake asked.

Tretheway carefully disentangled it from the tree. They examined it under the light: an approximately five-foot length of thick cord with several dirty grey feathers loosely knotted into it at uneven intervals.

"What is it?" Jake asked.

"God knows." Tretheway stuffed it into his pocket. "We'll look at it later. You'd better bring the bowl."

"Right." Jake picked it up. A low growling moan broke the silence, slowly at first, then climbed quickly to a loud, high-pitched steady scream.

Jake dropped the bowl. "What the hell's that?"

"Easy," Tretheway said. "It's the all clear. Let's go home."

Chapter Three

Although the war was far from over, there was a hint of optimism in the air. The Russians were demanding the surrender of the encircled 6th German Army at Stalingrad; Rommel's forces were retreating into Libya; RAF Bomber command had carried out devastating raids on German-held cities and, in the Pacific, US Marines were well into their retaking of Guadalcanal. All this, coupled with the thousands of miles Fort York was from the actual fighting, lent less urgency to the ARP meeting on the following Saturday.

Tretheway and his staff had spent two days going over and evaluating Fort York's first full-scale blackout. In general, it was considered a success. There had been no serious injuries or major foul-ups. The population of Fort York, influenced by the sobering thought that one day this might not be a practice, entered the exercise in the proper spirit.

On the Friday, Tretheway received a call from Police Chief Zulp.

"Tretheway."

"Sir." Tretheway recognized the low, gravelly voice of his superior.

"Good job. Well done."

"Thank you, sir."

"Hear it went well."

"Pretty good."

"No problems. No lights. Except that one."

"Sir?"

17

"The marsh. The light on the ice."

"Oh."

"You looked into it?"

"Yes, we..."

"Gas."

"Pardon?"

"Gas," Zulp repeated. "Marsh gas. St. Elmo's Fire. Wouldn't make too much of it."

"Right." Tretheway paused. "We're having a meeting Saturday night of the west-end Wardens. Just to sort things out."

"Where?"

"At our place. Addie thought we could combine business with a little pleasure."

"Good thinking. Take people's minds off the war. Nazis. Rationing. Marsh gas. Sorry I can't make it. Me and the Missus have tickets to something."

Tretheway smiled.

"Give my best to Addie."

"Yes sir." Tretheway hung up.

Adelaide Tretheway was only slightly smaller but much prettier than her brother. She'd quit England in the early twenties to follow him across the ocean to Canada. They had settled in Fort York, a mid-sized industrial city at the western end of Lake Ontario. With a small inheritance she shared with Tretheway, Addie bought a large, rambling three-storey house in the west end close to Fort York University and turned it into a respectable boarding house. Most of her tenants were Arts or Theology students. Her star boarder, of course, was Jake. Tretheway had his own private large room and oversize bathroom facilities on the second floor.

The Tretheways' Saturday night euchre parties had grown in popularity over the years, with good reason. This Saturday the aroma of Addie's freshly baked bread was the first thing that attacked the senses. An applewood fire crackled in the fireplace. On its hearth, Fat Rollo, Addie's longhair black cat, lay noisily purring beside Fred, the neighbor's misnamed twelve-year-old female labrador. The disciplined conversation of students hummed against the background of music from "Your Hit Parade."

As usual, Addie had made platesful of sandwiches to go with the pop and beer cooling in the two ice boxes. Tretheway's special Molson's Blue quarts were cooling on the back verandah. Jake, Addie and Beezul, with the help of Bartholomew Gum, set up the card tables and chairs around the irregularly shaped common room next to the kitchen. A large four-by-eight-foot blackboard rested on an easel beside the head table. On it, Gum had drawn, crudely but clearly, a map of the west end of Fort York and Coote's Paradise showing all the blocks the Wardens patrolled on Wednesday evening.

Bartholomew Gum was an old friend of the Tretheways; he had grown up with Jake and shared in some of their adventures. Since the age of eight he'd stared with colourless eyes through rimless glasses and fought baldness. He lived with and supported his mother in a house not far from the Tretheways. His mother and his bad eyes were enough to keep him out of the armed forces. Gum had been a City Alderman for the last ten years and and Air Raid Warden since the beginning of hostilities. Wherever he went, he was early.

Zoë Plunkitt was even earlier, ostensibly to set up her table for taking minutes by shorthand, but Beezul thought it was out of guilt. "Probably to make up for being stuck in the snow and missing Fort York's first blackout," he said.

Miss Plunkitt was, as usual, plainly but tastefully dressed. Her thin, wiry frame, well suited for fashionable clothes, belied her physical strength and conditioning. She walked a lot, played some golf, sailed enthusiastically and once a week taught self-defense for ladies at the downtown YMCA. Her teeth were straight and even, her head erect. An intense look, combined with heavy eye makeup and frequent blinking, gave anyone talking to her the mistaken impression that she was listening with interest.

Garth Dingle also arrived early. A year ago, he'd become a resident of Fort York, and, shortly after that, one of the more popular Air Raid Wardens in the west end. Garth was head professional at the Wellington Square Golf and Country Club.

Jake had played golf off and on, but not seriously, for years. In 1941, he'd treated himself to a full membership at the venerable WSGCC located just outside of Fort York. In fact, from a number of the raised tees, you could look across Wellington Square Bay and see the smoke stacks of Fort York's industrial complex pumping black and grey clouds into the air in aid of the war effort. Jake was a mediocre but knowledgeable golfer, held no one up and adhered faithfully to the spirit of the game. On the few occasions when he attended the club's social functions, Addie and Tretheway usually accompanied him; and sometimes, just Addie. It was here he'd met Garth Dingle.

The head pro was a big man (by Jake's standards, not Tretheway's) with a bigger laugh. His weathered face showed permanent smile wrinkles and his eyes squinted continuously through smoked prescription glasses as though appraising his next shot. When he wasn't using his gnarled but sensitive hands to drive golf balls a straight and true country mile, he re-built things, like golf vehicles. Garth had reduced a 1920's vintage electric car to chassis, steering wheel, dashboard and batteries; he'd added a leather bench seat, oversize airplane tires and a bag rack. In this contraption, nicknamed 'Garth's Cart' by the members, he would hum over the course inspecting greens and bunkers, chase young aspiring, but trespassing, Byron Nelsons off the links, tactfully prod slower players along and, when he could, play a round of golf by himself in under two hours. He also rebuilt golf clubs.

This Saturday he'd delivered Jake's refinished woods, a gift from Addie, that Jake had scruffed up over two seasons. The two were hefting and admiring the gleaming persimmon heads. Tretheway watched them. He wondered how two grown men could spend that much time discussing golf sticks, let alone the additional time it took to play the game itself when there were more sensible, manly sports to participate in such as the hammer throw. His thoughts were interrupted by the arrival of the other ARW's.

Squire Middleton and Cynthia Moon arrived at the same time, but not together. They shared a quiet knock and waited. No one came to the door.

The Squire, as he was erroneously known, (his mother had christened him Squire) looked quizzically at Cynthia. His eyes were too small and too close together, but his thick, horn-rimmed glasses made them look owlish. An Irish walking hat covered his bald pate while a heavy tweed overcoat protected his smallish frame. Slung over his shoulder, a worn, leather school bag held his ARW literature and the tools of his trade as a street car conductor.

Cynthia Moon smiled pleasantly back at him and shrugged her wide shoulders. A bulky, black-fringed shawl that could have covered a large banquet table, was wrapped several times around her matronly upper body. Beneath it was an ample batik skirt she'd made and dyed herself. Her substantial legs disappeared into comfortable ankle-high running shoes.

"Hi." Mary Dearlove stepped up to the low verandah and politely pushed between them. "Have you knocked?"

They both nodded.

Mary knocked loudly and opened the door. "After you." She stepped back.

Her voice always surprised people—small, almost babylike. It didn't go with the impeccable makeup, perfect hairdo, matching full-length mink coat, hat, overshoes, and especially the clear blue eyes, pleasant enough at first, but with a promise of flint.

"You've both been here before," she clucked. "You just knock and go in. It's that kind of place."

The Squire and Cynthia Moon scampered in guiltily. Addie met the trio in the front hall. She greeted them and directed the hanging up of coats.

"Everybody here, Addie?" Mary Dearlove patted her hair into place and smoothed the front of her unwrinkled blouse.

"Almost," Addie said. "Patricia Sprong called. She'll be late. Band practice. There's still, let's see... Warbucks." She smiled. "Tremaine Warbucks."

Everybody smiled when they thought of Tremaine Warbucks. To some, who remembered his smiling eyes, his thin lips always turned up optimistically and the pithy bits of helpful information he freely offered, it was a genuine affection. To others, who took note of his gangly, stooped posture, his ill-fitting, unmatched clothes and the annoying pieces of useless information he constantly gave, the smile was less kind.

Someone knocked at the door. Before Addie got there, Tremaine Warbucks pushed in. He affected a grey, spiky, Amish-style beard with no moustache.

"Speak of the devil," Addie said.

"Good evening, Addie." Warbucks handed Addie his hat, coat and cane on his way through the hall. Tretheway tapped his large ceremonial night stick against the hard edge of the card table. Everybody quietened down and found a seat. Zoë Plunkitt sat at a table beside Tretheway and Beezul, her pencil poised, her eyes blinking. Jake found a comfortable spot on the arm of Addie's easy chair. The rest arranged themselves in the uneven arc of card chairs with their backs to the fire.

"I think we can call the meeting to order," Tretheway announced. He had spent Thursday and Friday with Jake, Beezul and, most of that time, Zoë Plunkitt, listening to the reports of other ARW groups that covered the rest of the city. The group captains, twelve in all, had reported nothing out of the ordinary for a wartime blackout. Some lights shone where they shouldn't have, but were quickly extinguished when the owners were told. There was a friendly spirit of unity. Everyone knew who the enemy was.

The FYPD and Militia reported similar activities in the residential pockets spotted throughout the northern industrial section. Fort York Centre, East, Delta, Mountain, West and Southwest districts were much the same. There were a few ill-prepared citizens who had gone out for the evening and left lights on in homes and stores, but Tretheway promised they would all be spoken to.

Although Bartholomew Gum was the group captain for the West, Tretheway took a personal interest in his own residential area.

"Captain." Tretheway looked at Gum. "Do you want to start?"

Gum stood up and cleared his throat self-consciously. He opened his notebook. In his position he had to cover the whole of Westdale instead of the few specific blocks individual ARW's were responsible for. Gum had pedalled his heavy black bicycle up and down every street trying to meet with each warden. Nothing of great importance took place. The high point of his tour occurred while he was taking a short cut through a dark back alley: he noticed a lady in a well-lit upstairs bedroom window, oblivious to the blackout regulations, disrobing for the night. Gum ran into a fencepost and fell, scattering garbage cans and cats. By the time he had regained his flashlight, helmet and composure, the offending light had been turned off. This event was not in his note book.

The ARW's followed with their oral reports, one after the other. There was a monotonous similarity in each. They were a reflection of the individual character of each warden rather than an accurate chronicle of a wartime activity.

Mary Dearlove had taken down the names of more offenders than anyone. The most minute crack of illegal light was duly noted. She complained about a group of FYU students riding their bikes with uncovered lights. When she blew her whistle, they bolted. "I mean, there was profanity." She missed the license numbers in the darkness. Mrs. Dearlove also let Tretheway know that her helmet didn't fit and was so heavy it crushed her coiffure. And as the widow of a former member of parliament, she was not accustomed to tramping the streets at night.

Garth Dingle had taken down no names. According to him, there were no illegal lights showing on his block. And the only person he had met was a beat constable who, after recognizing the golf pro, had brought up the problems of his own swing. Despite his heavy coat and steel helmet, Garth willingly demonstrated several solutions by taking many harmless divots out of the snow with a five iron. It was not unusual for him to carry a golf club on an evening walk.

Squire Middleton too reported no real problems. He had reasoned with a few people about improper lights and they had complied peacefully. At one point, because his glasses had steamed up, he had mistaken the full moon shining through some overhead lacy branches for a verandah light. The Squire realized his mistake just after he had blown his whistle. This brought a sympathetic guffaw from the other

ARW's.

The only warden who thoroughly enjoyed herself was Cynthia Moon. She said it was because of the tides. "My cycle's always high at full moon. You know, love, Diana." But just in case, she had added a scarab amulet to her many decorative strings of beads, and had stuffed extra charms in the pockets of her baggy peasant skirt. Cynthia reported a pleasant round of confrontations on her darkened blocks. All was well, she said, except for the cats. When Tretheway questioned her, she explained that several cats had followed her during the evening. "One big black one. The leader. And three brainless. They're the familiars, you know." Cynthia Moon usually said something nobody understood, but that was, Tretheway thought, a small price to pay for knowing her.

The only warden Tretheway could have criticized was Tremaine Warbucks. His habit of button-holing people and plying them with sometimes interesting but usually irrelevant information took time. Warbucks would offer tips on things like the practical use of small penlights or how to calculate the energy it would take to boil Wellington Square Bay dry. Although he had the smallest block, he never finished his rounds. However, his report, up to a point, was clear and concise: there had been no infractions. But toward the end, Warbucks began to wander. He launched into his well-thought-out theory of how to win the war by starting the invasion of Europe with thousands of camouflaged hot air balloons. Tretheway was about to interrupt when Patricia Sprong came in.

"Sorry I'm late, all." Miss Sprong strode in humming her favourite hymn, "The Devil and Me". She wore her navy blue, red-trimmed Salvation Army uniform. "Great band practice." She stood, her sturdy but shapely legs apart, in front of the fire, warming her backside. Her lantern jaw jutted forward and her clear blue eyes appeared even more luminous against the deep windburn of her face. She walked daily in Coote's Paradise, rain or shine.

"Evening, Patricia," Tretheway said. "Why don't you give us your report now."

"Okay." She looked around the room. "Is it my turn?"

"Yes," Tretheway said. "Tremaine's just finished."

Tremaine sat down.

"Well, it was all very orderly," Patricia Sprong began. "A few violations. Most were forgivable. But I have some names here to report." She went on to describe an efficient patrol. As a professional major in the Sally Ann, Sprong tended to be harder or easier on offenders in direct relation to their wealth. All the names she handed in were well-to-do folk. The poor and meek she forgave. And Tretheway couldn't help but notice that, unlike Mary Dearlove, Major Sprong was no stranger to unlit streets or dark alleys.

"That's about it, then?" Tretheway looked around the room.

Everybody looked around the room.

"That's fine." Addie stood up and flicked some crumbs from her apron. "Perhaps some sandwiches would be in order."

"Good idea," Jake said.

"What about the lecture on sand bags?" Gum asked.

"And some beer," Addie finished.

"We'll do the sand bags later." Tretheway stood up.

For the next thirty minutes, everyone socialized. They made short work of the tasty, substantial sandwiches (most of the men washed theirs down with ale) and helped themselves generously to the apple tarts Addie had made after saving up food coupons for weeks. Her home-made dandelion wine moved slowly. Fat Rollo stole a tart, but Fred was blamed for it. Finally, everyone wandered back to their seats and waited for the meeting to continue.

"I thought we'd go right into, 'How to Fill an Efficient Sandbag'", Tretheway began. "Then perhaps a little euchre."

Agreeable murmurs were heard, except from Mary Dearlove. She had no objection to playing euchre; something else was bothering her.

"Just a moment," she said to Tretheway. "What about *your* report? I mean, we've heard a lot of rumours."

"About what?" Tretheway asked.

"The light," Miss Dearlove persisted. "The light on the marsh."

"Come clean, Tretheway," the Squire chided. "Who was signalling the Luftwaffe?"

"I heard it was marsh gas," Patricia Sprong offered.

"Corpse's candles?" Cynthia Moon said.

"A form of phosphorescence," Tremaine Warbucks stated. "Ignis Fatuus."

Gum giggled and Garth Dingle guffawed loudly.

"All right." Tretheway held his large hands up, palms out partly in defeat and partly to control the meeting. "Settle down."

He had told Zoë and Beezul about the light. Jake had been there. Gum knew about it. And then there were the people who had phoned in. So it was no secret.

"We saw this light," Tretheway said. "Just where it was reported. Definite blackout violation. Coming from Hickory Island. So we investigated."

"You mean you went out there?" Addie asked. "Across the ice?"

"That's right." Tretheway had their attention. "Not that far. Made it without incident." He looked sideways at Jake. "We ascertained that someone had built a fire. Never found anyone. A bowl of wax had overflowed and flared up. That was the light we saw earlier."

"Wax in a bowl?" the Squire asked.

"That's right."

"Was the bowl bronze, by any chance?" said Cynthia Moon.

"Could be."

"And *only* wax in it?"

"I think so."

"Where is it now? Could I see it?"

"All right." Tretheway nodded at Jake.

"I'll get it." Jake left the room.

"And there were some diagrams in the snow. Circles," Tretheway continued.

"What size?"

"One very large one around the fire. Then some smaller ones. And stars."

"Stars?"

"Pentacles, perhaps?" Warbucks asked.

"They were half-trampled out. As though someone tried to get rid of them. And some numbers."

"What numbers?" Cynthia Moon asked.

"One, six, nine, two."

"Don't understand that," Cynthia said.

Jake came back carrying a bowl and an envelope. He put the bowl on the table. Everyone crowded around. Cynthia scratched at its hardened wax contents, releasing an unpleasant aroma.

"Smells like sulphur," Beezul said.

"Brimstone," Cynthia corrected. "There," she said finally.

"What?" Tretheway peered into the bowl.

"A pin," she said. "And I'll bet there are more. Deeper down."

"What do you make of that?" Gum asked.

Cynthia Moon didn't answer. "Was there anything else?" she asked. "Anything?"

Jake glanced at Tretheway, who nodded. He emptied the envelope onto the table beside the bowl.

The knotted cord looked untidy, unclean. And the nine feathers tied into its multi-coloured length were misshapen or broken. On Hickory Island it was just a piece of string swinging from a leafless tree. Here, in Addie's comfortable common room, in the warm light of the fire, it appeared alien, almost evil.

Cynthia Moon gasped. "A Witch's Ladder!" She grasped the largest amulet hanging amongst her beads and turned away from the table. Her eyes suddenly went glassy and as round as coasters. She pointed to the back of the room. Then she screamed; a primeval echoing. At that moment, Fat Rollo struggled to his feet and bolted with surprising speed under the shaky card tables in the direction of Cynthia's accusing finger. On his dash, he bumped into, or at least brushed against, several pairs of legs. Zoë Plunkitt and Mary Dearlove screamed. Fred's hackles rose and she started to bark. Addie squeezed the breath out of Jake. Twenty-six pounds of charging cat rammed the French doors that separated the room from Tretheway's back yard. Cynthia Moon fainted.

Garth Dingle recovered first. "It was a cat," he shouted. "Looking in the window. Just a dumb cat."

Patricia Sprong confirmed Garth's sighting. "That's right. A striped cat. It ran away."

In the next five minutes things calmed down considerably. Beezul helped Cynthia Moon to the couch. Addie brought some brandy in from the kitchen.

"I'm sorry," Cynthia said finally. "But everything happened at once. Hearing about all those things. And seeing the bowl. And a cat looking in the window. At night. A death sign. . ."

"That's all right," Addie comforted. "Just take a sip."

Tretheway noticed that Cynthia Moon was clutching her amulet again. He had always thought of her, despite her eccentricities, as a solid, both-feet-on-the-ground person.

She painted unusual, abstract canvases; her clothes were different; she told fortunes with tea leaves or tarot cards for amusement only and dabbled in mysterious sciences almost as a lark, a harmless hobby. Perhaps, he thought, Cynthia Moon's knowledge of the occult was not as shallow as he'd first surmised.

"If you know anything about these things," Tretheway said kindly, "Maybe you'd like to talk about it."

Cynthia Moon nodded. Everyone waited.

"Well." She took another sip of brandy. "There are a number of things. They may sound silly alone. But all together. . ." She looked at Tretheway.

"Go ahead," he encouraged.

"The blackout was on the thirteenth, for a start. A full moon. Close to midnight. The witching hour. What you saw on the island sounds like an altar. A witch's or devil's altar. A place prepared for evil. For casting spells." Cynthia looked around the room. No one said anything for seconds, but it seemed longer. Then everybody tried to speak at once.

"Rubbish," Patricia Sprong said.

"Oh dear," Addie said quietly.

"You're not suggesting some sort of witchcraft?" Mary Dearlove asked. "In 1943?"

"You mean that Tretheway and Jake almost caught a witch?" Gum said.

"Can't remember the last one we caught," Garth smiled.

"Seventeen twenty-seven," Warbucks stated. "In Scotland. Janet. . .ah Horne, I think. They say she turned her daughter into a flying horse. Laughed when they threw her onto the fire."

"Oh dear," Addie said again, louder.

Tretheway glared at Warbucks. "Let Cynthia finish."

"Make fun if you like." Cynthia reached for the brandy again, then thought better of it. "But when I think of witchcraft, I think of a religion. The craft of the wise. Wicca. It began before Christianity and will be with us forever. Now, I know there's a certain occultism involved. A spirit world. An intangible, primitive dimension that no one in this room can explain." Cynthia looked around for an answer before she went on. "But it's a harmless, non-destructive form of witchcraft. In ancient tales, white witches have shrunk goitres, banished melancholy, staunched bleeding and even aided lovers in their quests. They've raised cones of power that have changed the paths of history." Cynthia stopped. This time, she had a good swallow of brandy. She rearranged her strings of beads. Everyone waited. "However, what we have here is no old-time religion. This smacks of sorcery. Black magic. Devil worship. Everything points to evil. The demon's circle. The pentacles. The perverted rosary with its nine feathers. A bronze bowl. Fire. The wax and the pins that I'm sure were stuck into an effigy before it melted. Image magic. Brimstone."

She stood up. Her eyes, glowing with enthusiasm and brandy, transfixed Tretheway.

"There was something out there. A witch. A wizard. A warlock. An impish presence. Bent on malevolent mischief." Her voice rose. "Perhaps to raise a storm. To spoil a crop. To poison a well. To make a pact with the devil." Cynthia's eyes dilated. Her body twitched slightly. Exhausted, she sat down heavily on the couch.

The fire crackled. Fat Rollo stretched out again. Fred whimpered softly in mid-dream. The quiet conversation of two student boarders was muffled behind the kitchen door.

"On the other hand," Tretheway cleared his throat, "It could have been some FYU students."

"Having a lark?" the Squire suggested.

"Possibly some secret fraternity ritual," Beezul said.

31

"Maybe divinity students on a research project," Mary Dearlove suggested.

"Or raising a little hell," Garth said. "Nothing wrong with that."

Everyone nodded except Cynthia Moon.

"Couldn't it have been something like that?" Addie asked her.

Cynthia stared into Addie's hopeful eyes. She realized everyone was waiting for her answer.

"Of course it could." Cynthia smiled. "I didn't mean to alarm anyone."

"I mean," Addie went on, "nothing happened really. No one was hurt, or anything."

"You're right, Addie," Jake said. "Let's have some sandwiches."

Addie brightened. A hum of conversation began.

"All right." Tretheway tapped his night stick on the table again. "We'll do the sandbag thing another night. I think we've covered everything."

"Except for the bat," Garth Dingle said, almost under his breath.

All talk stopped again. Cynthia's smile disappeared. Zoë blinked furiously. The worried look returned to Addie's face.

"The what?" Tretheway said.

"The bat," Garth repeated. He stood by the fireplace innocently kicking ashes across the hearth. Jake recognized his tone as the same one he used when he baited members of the WSGCC about an obscure rules infraction on the course. "The giant sliding bat that moved toward the light." He continued to stare at his feet. No one breathed.

Tretheway looked daggers at Jake. Jake stared straight ahead, his neck reddening.

"Jake?" Tretheway said quietly. Jake straightened up uncomfortably on the arm of Addie's chair. "Perhaps you'd like to answer this one?"

Jake stood up, glanced sheepishly at his boss and put his hands in and out of his pockets before he stammered his way into the explanation. By the time Tretheway had once again taken off across the marsh, most were smiling, some snickering. And when the great bat fell, everyone laughed. Even Tretheway had to smile.

The relief of laughter continued longer and louder than the story warranted. Tretheway noticed Zoë Plunkitt, handkerchief in hand, dabbing, trying to save her eye makeup from the running, hysterical tears. At the time, he put it down to the simple relief of tension.

Chapter Four

In the heart of Fort York's business section was a pleasant sward of parkland known as The Gore. It had evolved from a raw firewood market in 1860, with small spindly saplings, into a lush boulevard that split King Street for three downtown blocks. At the west end, a giant benevolent statue of Queen Victoria, guarded by sculptured lions, stared haughtily down on her people from a high concrete column. An inscription read, 'Queen and Empress/Model Wife and Mother'. At the other end, a lifesize copper replica of Sir John A. McDonald stood on a similar column flanked by two twenty-four pounder ship's guns from the War of 1812. In the centre of The Gore, a magnificent fountain, continuously spouted noisy but soothing jets of water around its three-tiered, circular design. Flowers and mature trees ran the length of the park.

Here, on warm summer afternoons, tired shoppers, layabouts, people waiting for buses and visiting servicemen rested, cooled off and contemplated their uncertain futures. On Saturday, February 13, about thirty minutes past midnight, The Gore was cold and deserted except for the dead rabbit.

"Tretheway's." Jake was first to reach the phone. "Hi, Wan Ho." Jake smiled into the receiver. "What's on your mind?"

As he listened, his smile vanished, his brow wrinkled. His

face assumed the worried, perplexed look it wore when his car wouldn't start.

"Just a minute," Jake said. "I think you'd better talk to the Boss."

It was an unusually quiet Saturday evening when the Tretheways had only one guest. Cynthia Moon had visited Addie in the afternoon to discuss the planting of an indoor herb garden and stayed on for dinner. The two sat now in the small front parlour comparing the merits of lemon balm and periwinkle. Tretheway half-reclined across from them in his oversize chair, puffing on a large cigar and reading the late edition of the *Fort York Expositor*. He was midway through a news report about a Canadian coastal command bomber scoring a direct hit on a Boche submarine when Jake came back from the phone.

"It's for you," Jake said. "Sergeant Wan Ho."

Tretheway grunted unhappily, not because he didn't like Wan Ho, but because he had to go through the ordeal of rising prematurely from the comfort of his easy chair. The other three strained sympathetically as they watched 280 pounds of the law push himself forward, ashes and newspaper rolling down his front to the carpet, and finally rise, puffing and red-faced, to his height of six foot five.

"Bloody chair." Tretheway left the room.

Addie looked a question at Jake.

"One of the boys found a rabbit in Gore Park," Jake offered.

"Hardly worth a phone call."

"In a tree," Jake went on.

"Alive?" Cynthia Moon asked.

"Jake shook his head.

"Oh dear," Addie said.

Nothing more was said until Tretheway came back into the room. He lowered himself into his chair, more easily than he had risen from it, recovered the newspaper from the floor and flipped through the pages looking for his U-boat story.

"Albert," Addie interrupted.

Jake winced at the use of Tretheway's given name. Tretheway grunted.

"What did the Sergeant want?"

"Nothing special." Tretheway found his story.

"What about the rabbit?" Addie persisted. "The dead rabbit in the tree?"

Tretheway looked at Jake. Jake smiled weakly.

Tretheway laid the newspaper on his chest. "One of the beat constables at Central found a rabbit hanging in a tree."

"Hanging?"

"By the neck."

"Now, what kind of person would hang a dead animal in a tree?" Addie asked.

"Addie," Tretheway paused. "They think it was alive when they hanged it." He paused again. "You might as well know. It was mutilated. Missing a foot."

Addie gasped.

"Left hind?" Cynthia asked.

"Yes." Tretheway looked at Cynthia Moon. "How did you know?"

"That's the one they usually cut off."

"They?" Tretheway said.

"Whoever performed the ceremony."

"Usually?" Addie said.

"That's considered the lucky foot."

"Now hang on, Cynthia," Jake interrupted. "Are you trying to tell us that some sort of ritual took place in Gore Park? In the middle of the night?"

"Probably midnight." Cynthia looked at Tretheway. He nodded.

Jake leaned back into the sofa. Addie fiddled with her

apron. Tretheway thought about Hickory Island but decided not to bring it up.

"What's so special about rabbits?" he said to Cynthia.

Theatrically, Cynthia covered the lower half of her face with a black shawl. Her voice dropped to a kind of growl. "Witches travel by night in the shape of hares."

Addie's eyes widened in alarm.

"Oh, Addie." Cynthia dropped her shawl and squeezed Addie's knee. "I'm only kidding."

Addie laughed nervously.

"Cynthia." Tretheway put his newspaper on the floor and leaned forward. "Honestly, if you know anything that might help. . ."

"All right. I shouldn't joke about it." Cynthia fumbled for her favourite amulet. She clutched it in both hands and stared at the ceiling with her eyes tightly shut.

Addie and Jake looked at each other, then at Tretheway. He swiftly stilled any potential interruption by raising a stubby forefinger to his lips. Outside, the February wind rose, flicking the frozen tips of the juniper bushes against the frosted parlour window panes. Fat Rollo waddled in silently and lay down at Cynthia Moon's feet.

"The evil eye," she began finally. "Malocchio. The basis and origin of the magical arts." Cynthia held her stone beetle at arm's length. "This is a talisman to ward off the evil eye. To attract a fascinator. A rabbit has a natural protection against Malocchio because it's born with its eyes open." She lowered her hands to her lap, still clutching the scarab. "And it's fast. Changes directions quickly. Stands up like a human. Destroys crops. The Ancients believed there were magical powers in rabbits' hind feet because they touched the ground ahead of the front feet."

Her voice dropped, and she continued slowly. "Hence, a left hind foot, cut off a freshly-killed rabbit at midnight becomes a powerful charm. . ." She stopped and checked her audience. She thought she had probably said enough. Jake and Addie looked hypnotized. Tretheway was biting his cigar. Cynthia carefully rearranged her beads. She coughed self-consciously. The loudest noise in the room was Fat Rollo's wheezing.

Jake leaned back and broke the silence. "How about some euchre? And some nice big cheese-and-onion sandwiches?" He smiled at Addie. Addie brightened.

"And perhaps some beer," she suggested.

Tretheway brightened.

Chapter Five

Mary Dearlove's husband, Ferdinand L. Dearlove, Member of Provincial Parliament, had died of natural causes in 1938. Even though there was enough money for her not to work, Mary decided to go back to her first love, her university major—Journalism. She wanted to be a police reporter. She finally landed a job on the *Fort York Expositor*, but because of her background—old family, private school, MPP's wife, etc.—the editor assigned her, logically, to the society desk. For the past few years, she had covered weddings, funerals for the locally famous, church teas, war bond extravaganzas and New Year's day levees for both the Royal FY Light Infantry and City Hall. Although she still harbored dreams of the big scoop, Mary Dearlove wrote an entertaining, intelligent society column. This month her assignment highlight was taking place on Saturday evening, the thirteenth; it was the Annual Fort York Policemen's Ball.

Addie had spent a rare afternoon at the beauty parlour and now, in the early evening, she stood before the hall mirror checking her coiffure. "Oh, dear." She tugged and pulled at the tight-fitting bodice of her new electric blue party dress.

"I don't know," she said to her reflection.

"Addie. You look great." Jake beamed with admiration. He looked over her shoulder at his own image; the dark uniform fresh from the dry cleaners, knife-edge crease in the pants, thin scarlet seam, black dress shoes and a touch of paddy green in the good conduct medal on his chest. His polished silver buttons sparkled against the deep navy of his tunic. He carried his hat and white gloves.

"Good-looking couple," Jake said.

Addie smiled.

"Where are my gloves?" Tretheway was banging cupboard doors in the kitchen. "They were here a minute ago. Now they're gone. Never mind. Someone put them on the ice box."

Jake and Addie exchanged glances. Tretheway entered the hall. "We should be going."

"We're late already," Gum said, rocking from one foot to the other with his coat on. He had walked over earlier as planned, to share a ride with the Tretheways and Jake in one of the several black-crested sedans pressed into service by the city for special occasions. Tonight, Jake was looking forward to driving a 1939 four-door Buick. He held the back door open for Addie. Gum eased in beside her. Jake, of course, slid behind the wheel while Tretheway squeezed himself into the roomy passenger seat—the only place he felt comfortable in a car.

"Got everything?" Tretheway stared straight ahead.

"Yes, sir." Jake patted the bulky paper bag beside him.

"Let's go," Tretheway said, still without turning his head.

The night was mostly clear but bitterly cold. A steady north wind swirled flakes of old and new snow across the windshield and long hood of the car. The wide white-walled tires crunched noisily as Jake guided the heavy machine through the ruts of the unploughed side streets.

The Policemen's Ball, the largest social function before the weather began to soften, was well attended; it gave everyone a chance to escape the winter blahs that seemed to hang on at this time of year and the persistence of police officers, Tretheway included, in selling tickets guaranteed a large turnout. This was apparent in the line-up of cars Jake joined in front of the Fort York Arms.

Tretheway looked in his side mirror. He noticed a car pulling up behind — a little bigger than theirs, a little grander, with an impressive city-crested flag flying on the fender.

"That has to be Zulp," Tretheway said.

Jake adjusted his rear-view mirror. "It is. The chief himself."

The lights blazed merrily under the ornate marquee as Tretheway and his party alighted from the luxury vehicle. Jake reluctantly handed over the keys to, he thought, a too-young, too-eager valet parker. They all waved at the car behind.

Luke Dimson was in his glory. What with opening and closing car doors, assisting matrons out of the deep pile seats and escorting them through the elaborate revolving brass doors, he hardly had time to blow his whistle.

The scene in the lobby was even more festive. People milled about shaking hands with old acquaintances they hadn't seen since the last ball and loudly greeting those they had talked to only yesterday. Police uniforms dominated, but mingled with the Armed Forces and, Tretheway quipped, "a sprinkling of firemen". All colourful dress uniforms, formal tuxedos and tails had been mothballed in deference to the war. Colours showed mainly in the ladies' attire. The blue of Addie's taffeta, the shimmering, fuchsia sequined dress that clung to the athletic body of Zoë Plunkitt, the wildly-hued peasant garb of Cynthia Moon and the golden, queenly radiance of Mary Dearlove's rustling silk suit showed up brightly against the sea of drab uniforms and business suits. Patricia Sprong wore the dark blue of the Salvation Army.

Music could barely be heard above the babble of conversation. It drifted down the wide circular staircase from the mezzanine where King Chauncey, accordion virtuoso, and his seven Merry Knights enthusiastically supplied music from the cavernous Crystal Ballroom.

"Why don't we go directly to the table?" Addie suggested.

"Good idea," Tretheway said. "I'll check the coats." He looked at Jake. "You watch the refreshments." Jake tightened his grip on the large paper bag.

Halfway up the carpeted stairway Jake stumbled. Tretheway's huge white-gloved hand cut quickly and painfully under Jake's armpit. It steadied him the rest of the way up.

"Now let's get to the table before you drop the bloody bag," Tretheway said. Addie frowned at her brother.

They pushed their way through the crowded mezzanine toward the main ballroom, waving and shouting greetings to old friends. Their progress was interrupted twice before they reached the table—once by Sergeant Wan Ho, who kissed Addie lightly on the cheek, shook hands all round and bowed ceremoniously in his best Charlie Chan imitation. Jake bowed back. Tretheway smiled. The three never missed a Charlie Chan movie and knew the detective's treasury of proverbs by heart. They often argued about which was the best picture and who made the best Chan. Tretheway favoured Warner Oland while Jake and Wan Ho preferred the later pictures with Sidney Toler. Tretheway rated Wan Ho as the most efficient plainclothesman on the Fort York force.

The second interruption was Dr. Nooner. The doctor, a Fort York native and the official Police Force physician, was a regular at Tretheways'. He served the same role with the Firemen, the FY Tagger Football Club, the elected representatives on the city council and the draft board. This way of life gave him little time for his own patients, which did not displease him. Doc Nooner greeted the Tretheway party warmly and , as usual, loudly.

He wagged the forefinger of one hand, while cradling a drink with the other, to warn them dramatically about the evils of drink and overeating. His head was moon-shaped and hairless; he had a chubby smile. And although he was much shorter than Tretheway, their potbellies still touched when they spoke to each other.

At the table Jake thankfully put down the unwieldy bag of refreshments.

"Anyone for a drink before I hide it?" he asked.

Tretheway winced. He still felt embarrassed at having to break the law. Because of the Province's archaic liquor laws, the hotel was not allowed to sell alcohol. (The hotel more than made up for loss of revenue by charging a king's ransom for ginger ale, soda water, ice, peanuts, party hats, toy horns, etc.) The venerable Fort York Arms, like all similar establishments, looked the other way while law-abiding celebrators guiltily slid their goodies under their tables. Jake's bag held a quart of Scotch for Tretheway, who had to forego his Molson's Blue as just too cumbersome, a mickey of Canadian rye for Jake and Addie, a small dark rum slipped in by Gum and two bottles of Addie's home-made dandelion wine.

The scene, with varying bag contents, was repeated at each table. And each table seated eight. At the Tretheways', Geoffrey Beezul and Zoë Plunkitt acknowledged their arrival with raised glasses of premixed martinis. The Zulps were to occupy seats seven and eight but were still socializing enroute. At the adjacent table, also filled because of Tretheway's aggressive ticket selling, were the six other ARW's. They were all seated except for Mary Dearlove, who was away ostensibly gathering tidbits for her next week's column. The remaining two seats awaited Doc Nooner and Sergeant Wan Ho.

King Chauncey squeezed life into his accordion as a signal for the start of a new dance set. The lights dimmed.

Chairs scraped back. The level of conversation rose expectantly as the men chose partners.

"Addie?" Jake stood up. "Would you care to..." he pointed at the dance floor.

"Certainly." Addie brushed past Tretheway. "Shouldn't you ask someone?"

"Eh?" Tretheway was pouring a drink.

"To dance," Addie said. "Just to be sociable."

"Well..." Tretheway stood up. The only lady at the table was Zoë Plunkitt. And it was obvious to Tretheway that Beezul and Gum weren't interested in dancing.

"Zoë?" Tretheway asked. "Would you care to dance?"

"I'd be delighted." With a slightly disapproving glance at the other two men, Zoë walked ahead of Tretheway to the already crowded dance floor.

When pushed, Tretheway had to admit that he enjoyed music. He liked to sing, listen to marches and some operas, didn't care for jazz but could be moved by a sentimental wartime ballad such as the one the band was now playing.

As one of King Chauncey's Knights warbled the lyrics of "When the Lights Go On Again All Over the World," Tretheway and Zoë Plunkitt began their spin around the floor. Although Zoë felt doll-like in Tretheway's terpsichorean embrace, her grip and manner said otherwise. Her coordination, coupled with Tretheway's peculiar grace— a grace that sometimes accompanies obesity— made the pair a pleasure to watch. Leather shoes slid rhythmically over the powdered hardwood floor. The slowly rotating mirrored chandelier spun diamonds of moving light over the fox-trotting couples, suggesting an aura of hypnotic fantasy. The war seemed far away, or at least romanticized into acceptability.

However, the next number was fast—"G.I. Jive." Tretheway suggested they sit down. On their way back through the crowd, Tretheway noticed that Zoë Plunkitt bumped into a couple of chairs, one of them at the Mayor's table. "What the hell," he thought. "It's a party."

"Tretheway." The Mayor waved.

"Mr. Mayor." Tretheway waved back.

"Would you and Miss Plunkitt care to wet your whistle?"

"Maybe later, your Honour." Zoë shook her head politely.

Joseph L. Pennylegion had worked his way up through the Fort York political system as a volunteer, alderman, and senior controller to his present post of mayor. As sometimes happens, his talents expanded with each succeeding office to more than fill the job. He was more or less thrown into competence.

His early history was obscure. He had appeared suddenly in the bewildering area of North American Prohibition as someone with money and influence. "Transportation," he would say if asked by reporters where his wealth came from, which was probably partly true. He was loyal to the Runyonesque friends who had shared his beginnings and now shared his table. They had names like Quick Roy, Fingers, and Worm. When the Mayor rode in his official limousine, they always followed him in a large black private sedan. In the world of municipalities he had the reputation of running a "tight" city.

Mrs. Pennylegion, too, had grown with her husband's career. Neither had much formal education but they were street-wise and possessed a blunt, sometimes vulgar, honesty that could be refreshing or shocking, depending on your viewpoint. She was overdressed; he was overweight and loud. His carrot-coloured hair, showing no grey, clashed violently with his flushed complexion. And they both used too much perfume or cologne, although now much more expensive brands than in the old days.

"Fine," Mayor Pennylegion shouted. "Come back later. I got champagne."

When they reached the table, Zoë Plunkitt took her matching sequined purse and left to powder her nose. Tretheway noticed that Mary Dearlove joined her on the way. The Zulps had finally arrived and were chatting with Bartholomew Gum and Beezul. Jake and Addie were still dancing.

Tretheway glanced at the next table. Garth Dingle was already wearing one of the party hats and amusing Patricia Sprong and the Squire. The Squire's refreshment bag sat on his lap. Tremaine Warbucks danced with Cynthia Moon and even from a distance could be seen talking without pause. Nooner and Wan Ho were still not in their seats. Mary Dearlove came back from the ladies' room and seemed to be visiting everyone. She danced with Dingle and Warbucks, shared rum with the Squire, soda water with Patricia Sprong and scribbled notes on an interview with Cynthia Moon. At one point, she even spent time walking around the perimeter of the dance floor, talking animatedly, arm in arm with Luke, the wandering doorman. At about ten o'clock, it was Tretheway's turn.

"Time for our dance, Inspector." Mary leaned over Tretheway's shoulder from behind. Addie pretended not to notice. A heady mixture of expensive perfume, freshly permed hair and mixed drinks wafted around Tretheway.

"My pleasure." He rose politely.

On the dance floor she performed well. But not quite as well as Zoë Plunkitt, Tretheway thought.

"Any juicy gossip for the column?" he asked, more for conversation than for interest.

"You'd be surprised." Mary Dearlove's words were ever so slightly slurred. And the look on her face reminded Tretheway of the look on Fat Rollo's face last summer when he was discovered holding a live baby bird between his paws.

"Oh?"

"I've come across a very interesting item."

"Like two ladies wearing the same dress?" Tretheway tried to keep it light.

"More than that. A secret. A deep, dark secret."

"You're serious, aren't you?"

"This could be my big story."

"At the Policeman's Ball?"

"It's more of a police story."

"You're not getting in over your head?"

"I can handle it."

"Well, if you need help...."

The music stopped.

"As a matter of fact, I might need your help. Tonight."

Mary Dearlove spotted Zulp approaching.

"When?"

"Later." Fat Rollo's expression appeared on her face again.

"Where?"

The music started up again.

"Come, come, Tretheway," Zulp blurted. "You can't hog all the beautiful women."

Mary Dearlove blushed as coyly as a middle-aged woman could.

"The Missus is waiting." Zulp looked at Tretheway.

"What?"

"Mrs. Zulp." Zulp jerked his head backwards, at his table. "Back at the table."

"Right." Tretheway had forgotten his annual must-dance with his superior's wife. Zulp and Mary twirled away.

Tretheway didn't remember much about dancing with Mrs. Zulp. He couldn't stop thinking of Mary Dearlove; about her clandestine manner, and about some of the puzzling comments she had made. What deep, dark secret, he thought. And what could he do to help?

Mrs. Zulp had stopped talking. She stared intently at Tretheway managing to focus on a spot some distance behind his head. Tretheway realized she was waiting for an answer.

"I see." He nodded his head and smiled. It appeared to satisfy her. She continued her thick-tongued monologue which gave Tretheway more time to reach back into his memory. One phrase nagged more at his worried subconscious than any other; two words that he turned over and over in his mind as he whirled perfunctorily around the floor—"witching hour."

"Thank you very much, Inspector." Mrs Zulp clapped her hands together decorously.

Tretheway jerked back to the present. The dance was over. "My pleasure, Mrs. Zulp." He joined in the applause. From Mrs. Zulp's benign expression Tretheway concluded that he must have nodded and smiled in all the right places during their conversation. He followed her on her unsteady passage back to the table.

The evening gained social momentum. Everybody wore a party hat except Tretheway. Addie's and Jake's matched, but only Addie's was becoming. Mrs. Zulp's hat twisted over one eye while the Chief, in metallic gold and purple, still managed to look intimidating. Beezul and Gum sported tasteful but festive models. Zoë Plunkitt had found a fuchsia, conical one with a sequined floppy brim that matched her dress.

"Albert, you don't have a hat," Addie said.

Tretheway shrugged.

"We'll find you one." She began to look around.

"Addie." Tretheway caught his sister's eye. "Don't worry about it."

Addie stopped looking.

By now, all attempts to hide the refreshments had gone by the board. Bottles, no longer full to the top, stood in the centre of every table for all to see, with white gloves abandoned beside them.

Tretheway overheard Garth Dingle tell a loud joke to Patricia Sprong—who had switched to white wine—and Cynthia Moon. They both laughed well before the punch line. He watched the Squire close his eyes gradually as he listened to a list of Warbucks's statistics. Mary Dearlove sat down for less than a minute before she disappeared into the crowd again. Doc Nooner and Wan Ho exchanged old anecdotes. Horns tooted tentatively all over the ballroom, rehearsing for the midnight release of balloons from the ceiling. The general noise level increased.

The drums rolled. "Ladies and gentlemen." King Chauncey announced as though introducing a prize fight, "The Paul Jones!"

Before the balloons were released from their nets, before the short speeches form the Mayor and Chief Zulp and before the final toast to the King that officially wrapped up the 1943 Ball, the highlight of the evening was the Paul Jones. A local hybrid dance, part grand march, part fast fox trot, part polka, but mostly square dance, it was the pinnacle of sweat-producing physical activity during the ball. Everybody took part.

Tretheway danced first with Patricia Sprong. She felt strong and capable, but not unfeminine, in his arms.

"I just love a Paul Jones," she said in anticipation.

"Gets the blood moving," Tretheway said.

"Good for the soul." She whirled Tretheway around exuberantly, or at least as much as anyone could whirl a two-hundred-eighty pound partner.

"Gentlemen, dance with the lady behind," King Chauncey chanted.

Tretheway released the Major, who began to whirl Beezul around. He, in turn, was claimed by Cynthia Moon. The music increased in tempo.

"Good party," Cynthia Moon shouted over the noise of her jangling costume jewelry.

They bumped into more couples now but nobody seemed to mind. Through the rising smoke and glittering reflections on the spinning revelers, Tretheway caught sight of Mary Dearlove dancing with Mayor Pennylegion. He remembered the cryptic message.

"Join in fours. Make a circle."

Tretheway and Cynthia obediently joined hands with Doc Nooner and Zoë Plunkitt.

"Skip to the right."

It was almost impossible to carry on a conversation during such wild activity. Tretheway lost sight of Mary Dearlove in the frenzied circling. Zoë Plunkitt squeezed Tretheway's hand as she smiled widely and skipped around the imaginary circle in time to the music. Cynthia Moon was just as restrained. Doc Nooner wheezed dangerously but still smiled.

"Everybody reverse."

Tretheway noticed with concern the bulging eyes and florid face of Doc Nooner as they all skipped in the opposite direction.

"You okay?" Tretheway shouted.

All Doc Nooner could manage was a weak smile. He continued to sweat and skip.

"Gentlemen, dance with the opposite lady."

Tretheway enjoyed the respite of the slower fox trot and he was sure Doc Nooner appreciated it even more.

"The good doctor's not in good shape," Zoë Plunkitt said.

"I know," Tretheway said.

"And he's so overweight."

Tretheway didn't answer.

"I mean, some men can carry it. Big men. With big frames. And still be in good shape."

"I suppose." Tretheway tried to hide his shortness of breath.

"It can be very attractive."

Tretheway noticed how effortlessly Zoë danced—she was as sprightly as she had been at the beginning of the evening. The diamonds of light flitted over her face and hair as they moved in time to King Chauncey's rhythm. But it was her eyes that Tretheway noticed more than anything; how they stared at him, unblinking, luminous, deep, bordered by dark makeup. He had seen that look before at an animal farm, in a soft rain, when a deer had wandered too close to the barricade—a doe, a wet-eyed doe...

"Grand March," King Chauncey shouted. "In fours."

Tretheway shook himself. Zoë Plunkitt began to blink. The music changed to fast martial. They joined the nearest couple—Addie and Garth Dingle.

"Great party." Garth spoke in his normal voice, which was loud enough to be heard above the din. He still had his party hat on. Addie smiled happily and squeezed her brother's arm.

"Now in eights."

Another foursome joined them, making eight abreast. Tretheway looked across the rank to see the Squire with Mrs. Pennylegion. An unusual pairing, he thought, but in a Paul Jones, anything's possible. Tremaine Warbucks and Mary Dearlove completed the eightsome. Mary winked at Tretheway.

"Make a big circle."

The ballroom immediately filled with rings of eight people, facing inward, hands joined, feet stomping in time to the music. Garth Dingle let out a yell he had heard in the latest Gene Autry movie. Mrs. Pennylegion screamed with glee. Others joined in. The music became louder.

"Now who..." King Chauncey looked around the room at the expectant faces during his dramatic pause.

"Who is...the birdie in the cage?"

This was the signal for the boisterous merrymakers to choose one of their eight to be in the centre of the circle—

their birdie—for the frenzied finale of the Paul Jones. In Tretheway's circle, he was picked.

"To the centre!" Chauncey and his group picked up their tempo and volume.

The remaining seven of each circle joined hands again and rushed toward the centre to form a cage of sorts over the hapless birdie, raising their arms and voices in a crescendo of squeals and shrieks. They repeated this several times at the command of King Chauncey.

"To the centre again!"

Some circles were more belligerent than others. They physically bumped their birdie. For the third year in a row, Mrs. Zulp was actually knocked off her feet. This did not happen to Tretheway.

"Once again!"

One group had zealously grabbed poor Luke as their birdie. With a wild smile he danced out of time to the music as they bumped and pushed him vigorously around the circle.

"For the last time!"

The last rush to the centre was the most spirited. Everyone yelped or squealed their loudest. The band's last crushing chord of trumpets, trombone, drum roll, cymbal crash and squeezed accordion signalled the climax. All arms rose in a final farewell to the birdie, the cage, and the Paul Jones for another year. Tretheway was lucky to hear Mary Dearlove say something over the racket.

He saw her lips move.

"What?" He bent over. She spoke in his ear.

"Midnight. Thirteenth floor."

Before Tretheway could answer, all came down with a final cheer. They all applauded themselves and the orchestra. The circles began to break up. Before Tretheway could get to Mary Dearlove, she disappeared once more into the milling crowd.

The next fifteen minutes were spent in recuperation. King Chauncey and his Knights took a well-earned rest. The lights spinning and sparkling over the crowd, became brighter. Most of the dancers returned to their own tables to re-fuel. Some visited other tables while others retired to the rest rooms for repairs,

"See Mrs. Zulp fell again." Garth Dingle sat beside Tretheway.

Tretheway smiled. He sipped Scotch from an oversize tumbler filled with ice.

"Third year in a row," Jake said.

"Do you suppose she's all right?" Addie seemed concerned.

"I think so," Beezul said. "Zoë and Cynthia went to the ladies' room with her.

"She's okay, Addie," Tretheway reassured his sister.

"Anyway," Garth nodded at Zulp, "the Chief's not worrying about it."

They all looked across the table. Chief Zulp sat quietly, his eyes glazed, both his gloved hands clutching a half empty glass of gin.

"Doesn't seem too concerned," Beezul observed.

"Even peaceful," Tretheway said.

"Too friendly with John Barleycorn," Garth giggled.

"Also the third year in a row," Jake said.

Even Addie had to smile. She looked around suddenly.

"Where's Mary Dearlove?"

"What's the time?" Tretheway said abruptly.

"Pardon?"

"The time. Addie." He pointed to her gold pendant watch.

"It's about twenty minutes before midnight. I think." She squinted at the antique numerals. "Maybe fifteen. I love this old watch but it's not reliable."

"Looks nice, Addie," Jake said.

"Let's go, Jake," Tretheway said.

"Eh?"

"Where are you going?" Addie asked.

"We have a little business," Tretheway stood up.

"We do?" Jake said.

Tretheway glared at Jake. Jake stood up. He smoothed the front of his uniform and adjusted his party hat.

Beezul assumed it was ARP business. "Can I help?" he asked.

Tretheway shook his head. "We won't be long. He started across the floor.

"Now don't miss the balloons." Addie looked at Jake. "That's at midnight."

Jake shrugged and hurried after his boss.

"I'll save you a red one," Garth shouted after them.

Jake caught up to Tretheway. "Where are we going?"

"Elevator."

As they jostled their way through the crowd, Tretheway told him what Mary Dearlove had told him, including her planned midnight rendezvous.

"Doesn't sound too ominous," Jake said.

"Maybe not," Tretheway said. "I just have a funny feeling about it."

Jake didn't comment further. He remembered that most of Tretheway's funny feelings were usually more than feelings and never humorous.

The elevator already held several hotel guests on their way to their rooms. The last one got off at the eighth floor.

"Floors, please," the elevator operator droned indifferently. She pushed the lever over to start the elevator upwards.

"Thirteen," Tretheway said.

"No thirteen."

"But I'm sure..."

The operator pointed to the numbers above the door

without speaking. Tretheway and Jake craned their necks and watched the indicator light pass through the circled numbers. When the elevator stopped, it was at twelve. The next number was fourteen.

"Maybe we should go to fourteen," Tretheway suggested.

"It's closed." She opened the door.

"Closed?"

"Roof Garden." A signal buzzed in the elevator. "I gotta go."

"Just a moment." Tretheway drew himself up to his full height and stared down at the operator. "Perhaps you should take a few minutes of your time to assist the Boys in Blue," he said loudly.

"Yes, sir." The bored look disappeared from her face.

"Now," Tretheway asked, "why no thirteen?"

"Tradition," she said. "No hotel has a thirteenth floor. Bad luck."

"Ah." Tretheway seemed satisfied. "But if there were a thirteenth floor, it would be...?" he pointed skyward.

She nodded.

"The Roof Garden?"

She nodded again.

"And it's closed?"

"Yes, sir. Only open in the summer. You know, dancing under the stars."

"I've been there with Addie," Jake said.

"Do you know Mrs. Dearlove?" Tretheway persisted.

"The newspaper lady?"

Tretheway nodded.

"Yes, I do. Brought her up here about five minutes ago."

"Just her? Nobody else?"

She nodded. "That's right."

Tretheway stepped out of the elevator. Jake followed. Tretheway stopped. "Where are the stairs?"

The operator leaned out the elevator. "Can't miss 'em."

She pointed down the hall. "But, like I say, they're all locked up."

Tretheway grunted. The buzzer sounded again. She looked at Tretheway.

"Go ahead," he said. "Thanks for your trouble."

"Any time." She smiled. "Anything for the Boys in Blue."

Tretheway and Jake watched the lighted elevator disappear downwards. They turned and walked briskly past the second set of dark elevator doors. Tretheway yanked open the heavy fire door and vaulted up the stairs, two at a time. Jake stayed close behind. Tretheway tried the upper door.

"Damn! Locked!"

"Just like she said."

"I know Mary Dearlove's out there," Tretheway said.

"How'd she get there?"

"Good question." Tretheway brushed past Jake and started down the stairs, again two at a time. He stopped abruptly. "How about the key?"

"Probably at the front desk," Jake said. "Downstairs."

"Logical. But we don't have time."

Tretheway strode back past the elevators toward a main corridor. He looked left and right. "There," he said. He pointed a finger towards the back of the building. Jake made out a red illuminated "Fire Exit" sign above a window. By the time Jake caught up to his boss, Tretheway had wrenched the paint-stuck window upwards. Cold air flowed into the hall.

"Go see what it's like," Tretheway said.

"Me?" Groaning, Jake stepped over the snowy sill. His shoes clanged on the strips of metal that formed the fire escape platform just below the window.

"What's it like?"

"Cold."

"You know what I mean."

Jake looked up. The outside stairway zigged upwards to

the right for half a storey, then zagged back to roof level.

"It looks okay."

"Good," Tretheway said. "Up you go."

"Aren't you coming?"

"Right behind you." Tretheway grunted as he scrambled over the sill.

Jake started up the metal stairs. The traffic on the ground looked like dinky toys.

"Don't look down," Tretheway said.

Just as Jake reached the landing, with Tretheway one step behind him, the first sonorous gong marking the midnight hour reverberated around them. Both men froze in their tracks. From the bell tower of the Fort York city hall a few blocks away, the notes sped through the wintry air of the March evening. Somewhere between the fifth and the sixth stroke they heard a scream, a wail, a banshee howl whipped and distorted by the wind, a screech that seemed to go on forever but that ceased suddenly at the last stroke of the hour. Tretheway and Jake still didn't move. Despite the weather, both were sweating.

"What the hell was that?" Jake said quietly.

"Don't know," Tretheway answered, just as quietly.

"The wind?"

"Maybe."

"Sounded like a scream."

"Probably a siren."

"Yeah," Jake said. "I'll bet that's it."

"Let's get on with it." Noticing the cold, they suddenly hurried up the stairs.

At the top, they encountered a small problem. The fire escape had been designed for people going down, not up. They wasted minutes climbing over the ice-and-snow-covered parapet to the roof. Tretheway pushed Jake over a slippery shoal.

"Where the hell are we?" Tretheway brushed dirt and

snow from his uniform. He noticed he had lost two buttons.

"At the back of the building." Jake pointed. "There's the Roof Garden."

Tretheway made out the silhouette of a four-sided pavilion with a peaked roof. The shadows cast by the evenly spaced arches cut into the walls, complicated and confused the image.

Tretheway started towards it.

"What's that?" Jake pointed left.

In the midst of the garbage bins, ventilator fans and other functional devices on the roof, was a larger structure about the size of a small hut.

"Must be the stairs."

"The door that was locked?" Jake said.

Tretheway yanked at the handle. "Still is." He rubbed dirt from his hands. "Not too elegant as entrance."

"Must be for the staff."

"How do the guests come up?"

"Elevators," Jake answered.

Tretheway looked at the ground. "I wonder who made those footprints."

Jake looked down. The footprints led away from the door. It was impossible to tell the old from the new because of the snow and the darkness.

"Better check them out," Tretheway said.

They followed the trail to the pavilion, up the few steps and through one of the arches to the inside. Even though they were out of the wind, it seemed colder. The footprints stopped when the snow did, at the edge of the summer-time dance floor.

"There are the elevators." Jake pointed.

"And the bandstand," Tretheway said.

Their voices echoed in the hollow interior.

"Looks bigger than I thought."

"And different than I remember," Jake looked around.

What he remembered was one balmy summer evening with Addie—music, dancing, a genial crowd, the clink of glasses and pleasant conversation. But now, the interior exuded that disturbed, even forboding, air of mystery that all people places have when they are empty; as though waiting for the next festive event and resenting any intrusion on its privacy. Jake shivered.

"Let's see if we can pick up these footprints," Tretheway said. "You go that way."

They split up and began to search the snowy perimeter just outside the walls. It didn't take long.

"Jake!" Tretheway shouted.

Jake's steps echoed as he ran across the dance floor toward his boss's voice. Tretheway stood under one of the arches.

"There." He pointed down.

There were enough footprints to confuse their direction and number, but they looked fresh. And they led about ten paces to a chest-high wall at the front edge of the hotel roof. On the flat top of the wall, just above the footprints, the fresh snow had been disturbed.

"Gawd!"

"You don't suppose. . ."

Their comments overlapped. They both ran to the wall and peered over.

"Careful," Tretheway warned.

A panorama of Fort York mid-winter night life displayed itself before them thirteen stories below. The few swirling snowflakes did not obscure the view. To their left, the foreshortened statue of Canada's first Prime Minister stood on the edge of Gore Park. Tiny car headlights probed the darkness. A street car rumbled by, bell clanging. No pedestrians were in sight.

"Looks quite normal," Jake said finally.

"Certainly does."

"You surprised?"

"Would've bet my pension someone, maybe Mary Dearlove . . ."

Tretheway let the name hang in the cold air. They stepped back form the wall.

"Maybe she wasn't here at all."

"Then what about the footprints?" Tretheway became agitated. "And the marks on the wall."

"Workmen?" Jake knew it sounded lame as soon as he said it.

"Damn it, Jake, at midnight?"

"Well, anyway," Jake tried to direct the conversation into calmer waters, "what do we do now?"

Tretheway glared at Jake. "We could start by taking off that bloody hat."

Except for a few dicey moments when Tretheway slithered back over the ice parapet to the fire escape, the trip downstairs was uneventful. Neither spoke. Tretheway wished to be alone with his dark thoughts while Jake sulked after putting his carefully folded party hat in his tunic pocket. The elevator operator honoured their silence. Back at the table however, they had to speak.

"Where've you been?" Addie began. "You've missed the balloons. Look at your uniform. It's torn." She looked at Jake. "You don't look so good either. Where's your hat?"

Jake's mouth opened but Tretheway spoke first. "Now Addie, settle down. It was unavoidable."

Jake nodded.

"Well, everyone was here gathering balloons," Addie said.

"I saved you both one," Garth smiled. "Red or white?"

"Everyone?" Tretheway said.

"Yes." Addie was adamant. "Everyone. Except you two."

"We were. . . " Jake started.

"On business," Tretheway finished.

Addie didn't answer.

"Addie," Tretheway said quietly, "this is important. When the balloons came down. At midnight. You're sure no one was missing?"

Tretheway had her attention. He also had the attention of the few others at the table. Beezul, Cynthia Moon and Zoë Plunkitt were listening. Garth stopped smiling. Sergeant Ho materialized beside Tretheway.

"Can anyone remember?" Tretheway said to the table.

The band started another set. About half the crowd made their way to the floor. A few had left home after the balloons. Others thought about it. 'God Save the King' wouldn't be played until one a.m., an hour later than usual—a special dispensation to FY's finest, the war and the liquor laws. But the party was winding down.

"We were all here." Beezul spoke first. He indicated everyone at the table. They all bobbed their heads in agreement.

"Gum was with me," Garth said. "But I didn't see Mrs Zulp."

"She was in the washroom," Cynthia Moon said, "throwing up."

"What about the Chief?" Tretheway asked.

"I don't think he's moved for over an hour." Wan Ho glanced at Zulp who was still sitting in front of his gin.

"Tremaine and Pat Sprong kept me company," Addie said with an edge to her voice.

"Doc and the Squire were with me." Wan Ho said.

"No one else you can think of?" Tretheway led them.

"The mayor and his wife were chasing balloons. Together," Cynthia Moon offered.

Tretheway waited.

"Mary Dearlove," Addie said to the table.

"What about her?" Tretheway asked.

"She wasn't here."

Tretheway looked at Jake. "Anybody see her?"

Everybody exchanged glances, then shook their heads.

"And where is she now?" Addie looked around.

"Dancing?" Zoë said.

"Maybe still gathering news," Cynthia suggested.

"Or on a secret tryst," Garth said.

Everyone stared at Garth.

"She's over twenty-one," he added defensively.

"You're quite right," Addie said. "Whatever she's doing, it's her business."

"Anyone for a martini?" Beezul asked.

"Don't mind if I do." Garth accepted.

Tretheway reached for his Scotch. They began to chat about other things.

After the last dance and the anthem, everyone was ready to go home. Most were smiling in recognition of another successful Policemen's Ball. The remaining refreshments were gathered up by their owners. Beezul's shaker was dry, the Zulps' gin was long gone and Jake's rye bottle and Gum's rum were dead soldiers on the table. Addie packed Tretheway's half bottle of Scotch and the two untouched bottles of her wine.

"I see the wine moved slowly again." Jake winked at Tretheway.

"I think this is the third year we've brought the same bottles," Tretheway said.

Addie ignored them.

As Tretheway and Jake struggled into their bulky winter coats, Wan Ho sidled up between them, and spoke quietly.

"I had my suspicions back there about Mary Dearlove. You two sure you're not holding back?"

"Ah," Jake said. "Good detective like good wine."

"Ah," Tretheway repeated. "Get better with age."

"Thank you so much," Wan Ho bowed.

Tretheway and Jake smiled.

"Honestly now," Wan Ho said. "If I can do anything to help."

Tretheway reached out and took Wan Ho's upper arm, in a firm but friendly grip. "In good time," he said.

On Sunday morning Addie vacuumed and dusted the house with the help of two willing student boarders. Jake appeared later. He went straight outside to shovel the four-to-five inches of snow that had fallen overnight. Tretheway slept in longer than anyone, but tidied up his own quarters before he came down for a late substantial breakfast. In the afternoon, he took his customary walk in Coote's Paradise. This time, Jake, Gum, the Squire and, as usual, Fred the Labrador went with him. Fat Rollo watched disdainfully from his place in front of the fire as the group marched out the front door into the sunny but wintry weather.

They skirted the university property and entered the woods by the Chegwin trail. At the south shore they headed west toward the beginnings of the old Desjardin Canal. For the next two hours, they saw rabbits, field mice, ground hogs, two chipmunks and countless squirrels which had left their nests to enjoy the March sun. Jake and Gum, former King's Scouts, identified the tracks of deer and foxes but saw none. Birds were plentiful: they saw starlings, blue jays, crows, circling hawks and had one spectacular sighting of a scarlet male cardinal against a sunlit snowbank. A small number of other congenial hikers shared their woods, but mostly they had the trails and hills to themselves.

Tretheway set a rigorous pace. Often he had to wait for the others to catch up. And near the end of their walk, they all had to wait for the Squire's breath to come back and his stitch to recede. Fred covered four times the distance of everyone else.

Back at the house, Tretheway pitched into making dinner. Earlier he had put a large roast of beef—a product of their pooled meat ration coupons and a friendly grocer—into the oven. The tantalizing aroma already pervaded the lower floor of the house. Now potatoes were added, large turnips and cabbages set to cooking and a generous dash of Tretheway's favourite curry for the gravy. It was his custom to cook Sunday dinner. He favored simple fare, English style, competently cooked with large servings—a gourmand's delight.

Everybody enjoyed the satisfying meal, except for the Squire. He picked at his food and said he was still recovering from the pain in his side, but Gum more than made up for him. And the student boarders ate as if they were going into hibernation.

After their guests had left and the students had returned to their studies, the Tretheways and Jake rounded out their day in the quiet of the small parlour. Tretheway sat in his oversized chair, feet stretched out, eyes half closed, puffing contentedly on a large cigar while Jake and Addie enjoyed some tea. Fat Rollo snored in front of the small parlour fire.

They turned the radio on at eight to laugh with Charlie McCarthy and his country cousins. A half-hour later their mood changed to pleasurable fear with "Inner Sanctum". They were brought back to reality at nine o'clock by Walter Winchell and the war news, but returned to humorous fantasy when Fred Allen took them on his weekly trip down Allen's Alley. At ten Jake perked up when the hockey game started. Addie said goodnight and retired. Tretheway turned the game off at eleven to hear "The Hermit's Cave." Jake said good night. When a live Benny Goodman show came on, Tretheway lit another cigar and leaned back in his chair. He didn't like that kind of music but he found it great background for contemplation. For the next while, he blew thinking smoke rings and carefully went over the events of Saturday night.

At midnight, as usual, he stoked the coal furnace, made the rounds checking windows and doors and patted Fat Rollo on the head hard enough to make him wake up, blinking, and stop snoring. On his way through the kitchen, Tretheway automatically pulled a quart of Molson's Blue from the ice box. He popped its cap off on the way upstairs to his quarters.

In the late afternoon, Monday, after an ordinary work day that held no surprises, Tretheway sat at the kitchen table with the *Fort York Expositor* spread out before him. He still had his uniform trousers on, but had changed into slippers and one of his many emblazoned sweat shirts. This one said, blue on white, "1928 Niagara Falls Police Games. Record Hammer Throw". Addie busied herself preparing roast beef leftovers while Jake struggled with the full pan of water under the ice box.

"How's the war news, boss?" Jake carefully carried the pan over to the sink.

Tretheway turned back to the first page. "'*Empress of Canada* claimed torpedoed again'," he read the headline.

"That's the fourth time she's been sunk," Jake chuckled.

"'Biggest Battle of Tunisian Campaign'."

"I think Monty's making his move," Jake said.

"'Essen all but destroyed by RAF'."

"For heaven's sake, Albert," Addie said. "Didn't anything nice happen?"

"Not on the front page, Addie," Tretheway said.

"Anything on the Policemen's Ball?" Jake asked.

"That's right. It should be in tonight." Tretheway started leafing through the paper.

"It's not there," Addie bit her tongue.

"Eh?"

"There's no report from Mary Dearlove."

"How do you know that?"

"Someone told me," Addie lied. "I forget who." She knew Tretheway didn't like anyone opening the paper before he did.

"Oh?" Tretheway looked at Addie.

"Maybe we should call the *Expositor*," Jake said hastily.

"Good idea." Tretheway thought for a moment. "First thing tomorrow." He turned to the comics.

They found Mary Dearlove the next morning.

True to his word, Tretheway was on the phone to the editor of the newspaper when the commotion started. He had just found out that Mary Dearlove hadn't handed in her column Monday morning, and hadn't phoned in with any excuse, which was unusual, the editor and Tretheway agreed, because she was just as fussy about punctuality as she was about her appearance.

"There's something going on out there," Jake shouted from the front of the office.

Tretheway thanked the editor hurriedly and joined Jake at the window almost before Beezul and Zoë did. He looked over the heads of the trio as all four craned to the right. A small crowd had gathered in a ragged circle around someone on the sidewalk close to the main hotel entrance.

"Someone's down," Jake said.

"A fall?" Beezul asked.

"I think it's Luke Dimson," Zoë said.

"Let's get out there." Tretheway pressed forward. Jake was forced to open the door to relieve the pressure. Outside, although the temperature was rising under a warming sun, a bitter wind made them uncomfortable without their coats. At the scene, Tretheway pushed through the ring of onlookers and squatted down beside the prostrate doorman. He was semi-conscious, arms and legs twitching, eyes rolled back in his head, but breathing. Anything he said, or tried to say, was unintelligible.

"Is he okay?" Jake peered over Tretheway's shoulder.

"I don't know," Tretheway said. "Anybody see what happened?"

"I did, Inspector." Frank the barber, who used to be called Francisco but had changed his name because of the war, squatted on the other side of Luke. He wore the white short-sleeved coat of his trade.

"I was looking out of my window," Frank pointed over his shoulder unnecessarily—Tretheway and most of his friends were regular customers—"when Luke became upset. Excited. Jumping up and down. Blowing his whistle. And pointing."

"Where?"

"Up. At the sky. Or the hotel."

"At what?"

"I couldn't tell from where I was. I ran right out. Tried to settle him down. Couldn't. Then he just went down."

"Did he say anything?"

"Yes."

There was a pause.

"Well?" Tretheway asked.

"I'm trying to remember," Frank said. "I want to get it right."

Sirens sounded in the distance. A beat constable arrived.

"'She didn't do it'," Frank said.

"That's it?" Tretheway said.

"What's it mean?" Jake asked.

"'There's one too many'," Frank said.

"One too many what?" Tretheway became impatient.

"No," Frank said. "Luke said that too."

"Just a minute." Tretheway settled down. "Let's get this straight. Luke said. 'She didn't do it', then, 'There's one too many'?"

Frank nodded. "Then he fell."

Tretheway stood up, relieving his leg cramps and moving aside for the ambulance attendants. They checked Luke over quickly, determined no immediate danger and whisked him professionally off to Fort York General. The beat constable moved the crowd along.

Tretheway stood, arms folded, almost meeting across his girth, staring up at the tall building.

"He was staring up there, Frank, was he?"

"That's about it." Frank looked over his shoulder. "I got customers." He disappeared inside his shop.

"It's cold. I'm going in." Beezul left.

"Me too," Jake said.

"Jake," Tretheway said. "Not just yet."

Jake stuck his hands in his pockets and followed his boss's gaze. Zoë stayed too.

"'She didn't do it'," Tretheway mused. "What do you suppose that means?"

The three continued to stare skyward.

"'There's one too many'," Tretheway went on. "One too many what?"

"Windows?" Jake suggested.

"Birds," Zoë offered. "Maybe nothing to do with the building."

"I don't think so." Tretheway's eyes traversed the hotel's front slowly from left to right; then back again, higher—like a typewriter, Jake thought.

At a level well above the high-ceilinged mezzanine, where red brick met the grey concrete base of the hotel's facade, a decorative ledge graced by evenly spaced gargoyles ran around the perimeter. Tretheway stopped suddenly, as though the typewriter had jammed.

"See anything?" Jake tried to pinpoint Tretheway's target.

"Nip into the office for a pair of binoculars," Tretheway said without taking his eyes from the building.

Jake left.

"What is it?" Zoë asked.

"Not sure." Tretheway turned and looked at Zoë Plunkitt. Her eyes were wet and unblinking. She trembled. "Maybe you should go inside."

"I'm all right," she said. "Just cold."

Jake reappeared. Tretheway snatched the binoculars from him. Jake felt glad that he hadn't put the strap around his neck.

Tretheway wiped the condensation from the eyepieces and snapped them to his eyes. As he slowly swept the grey architectural band, the gargoyles sprang into focus, one after the other. Just enough of the wind-whipped, melting snow had fallen from the ugly mythical creatures to reveal wrinkled misshapen features carved years ago by talented stone masons. Tretheway reached the spot he had been seeking and refocused the binoculars. Except for the snow, Mary Dearlove's coiffure was as immaculate as when she'd left for the ball. Her wide-open eyes gazed blankly. And her red lips grimaced in a frozen scream as hideous as any of her malformed concrete neighbours.

Tretheway lowered the binoculars.

"Gargoyles," he said. "One too many gargoyles."

Feverish activity filled the next two hours. The deceptively simple task of removing Mary Dearlove required a combination of police, medical personnel, hotel staff and a hook and ladder swarming with firemen. With the addition of the *Expositor*'s photographers and reporters, curious onlookers and Chief Zulp shouting needless commands, the pandemonium continued at fever level.

The body, stiff from death and hours in below-zero temperatures, proved unwieldy. And the ledge was slippery; practically inaccessible from a window. It had been designed for gargoyles, not for the cumbersome hip boots of the firemen.

Finally, they freed Mary Dearlove from her resting place. A strange silence fell over the throng as two firemen carried her down the aerial ladder into the dark privacy of the coroner's vehicle.

Tretheway watched stiffly; so did Jake and Beezul. Zoë Plunkitt cried.

"We need a talk," Tretheway said.

Everyone waited.

"Jake. Get hold of Wan Ho. And Doc Nooner. We'll meet tonight. Eight o'clock. At our place."

Jake scribbled in his notebook.

"Can I help?" Zoë asked.

"I'm free," Beezul offered.

Tretheway shook his head. "Not yet. But thanks, anyway."

They met in the parlour. Addie set out a fresh service of tea and several heavy slabs of the yellow cake with yellow icing that Tretheway favoured. She punched up a few cushions, patted Fat Rollo, and left, sliding the double doors closed behind her.

Tretheway started the meeting, "Thanks for coming. The first thing I should do is tell you two about a conversation I had with Mary Dearlove Saturday night. He looked at Jake. "And then, what we did after that."

"Instead of catching balloons," Wan Ho said.

"That's right." Jake smiled.

"All I ask is that you hold all your questions until I'm finished," Tretheway said.

He gave a concise but adequately detailed account. It began with Mary Dearlove's early evening innuendoes and ended with the two dishevelled law officers back at the party table.

When Wan Ho was sure Tretheway had finished, he started the questions.

"Is that why you wanted to know who was missing? When

we were catching the balloons?"

Tretheway nodded.

"And no one was missing?"

Tretheway shrugged.

"You went up the fire escape? At night?" Doc Nooner said. "Wasn't that dangerous?"

"No," Tretheway said. "A piece of cake."

Jake looked straight ahead.

"That puts a different light on it," Wan Ho said.

"In what way?" Tretheway asked.

"Right now the investigation has Mary Dearlove with too much to drink, going into a room on the twelfth floor, opening the window to clear her head and falling out. An accident. Simple as that."

"Which room?"

"Probably one of the party rooms on the twelfth."

"How'd she get in?"

"Could've been open."

"And nobody saw her?"

"Everyone was on the dance floor."

"You don't believe that." Tretheway shook his head. "But I suppose that's the official conclusion of the Investigation?" Everyone knew "the Investigation" was a synonym for Zulp.

"In all fairness," Wan Ho said, "up until now no one, including Zulp, had any reason to go on the roof. And even now. . ."

"What about the tracks?" Jake said.

"If I remember," Wan Ho said, "it snowed later that night."

"No tracks," Tretheway admitted.

"And you really didn't see anything," Wan Ho persisted.

"All right," Tretheway said. "In that case, let's keep this meeting unofficial. Just between the four of us."

"Or five." Jake looked at Fat Rollo.

"More like five and a half." Doc Nooner poked Fat Rollo's

stomach. Fat Rollo hissed.

"Your turn, Doc," Jake said. "Can you add anything?"

"How about the autopsy? Anything we don't know?" Tretheway said.

"There were a couple of things," Doc Nooner began, "but the body itself held no surprises. Its condition, broken bones, contusions, was consistent with a fall from that height. Killed instantly. No other wounds. However. . ." He paused. "Her left hand was tightly clenched. Took us a while to open it. To see what was in it."

"And?" Tretheway said.

"A rabbit's foot."

"Eh?"

"And it wasn't any cute little key chain. Hacked right off."

"Could it be the one from the Gore Park episode?" Tretheway looked at Wan Ho.

"Could be," he said.

"And what did the Investigation make of that?" Jake asked.

"That Mary Dearlove was very superstitious."

"News to me," Tretheway said.

"I can't imagine Mary Dearlove keeping an animal's dirty leg around," Jake said.

"You said two things, Doc," Tretheway said.

"Yes," Doc said. "Probably not important. But," he pointed at Tretheway, "you asked. She had a substance on her face. And arms, upper chest. Not too much of it. But noticeable."

"Substance?" Tretheway repeated.

They waited.

"Lard."

They waited again.

"Lard. Shortening. Chicken fat. We haven't put it under the microscope yet, but we're pretty sure."

"I'm not even going to ask what Zulp said about that one," Tretheway said.

"Exhaust fan," Doc explained. "There's a kitchen exhaust fan not far from where the body landed. Maybe some. . ."

"Oh, come on," Tretheway scoffed.

"You got a better explanation?" Doc Nooner looked around. "Anyone?"

No one answered. Jake scratched Fat Rollo and started him purring. Wan Ho poured tea for everyone. They polished off the yellow cake. Tretheway ate most of it.

For the rest of the meeting they cleaned up details. Luke was in shock. He was under sedation but would recover, Doc Nooner said. Zulp considered the case closed. He said it was a terrible thing. And that there should be something done about excessive drinking at official occasions, a recommendation that would be long forgotten by the time of the next Policemen's Ball.

At the meeting's end, Tretheway lit a cigar.

"Gentlemen," he said, "we've lost a good friend in Mary Dearlove." He took a few puffs. "But she's given us something to think about."

They adjourned to the kitchen.

Chapter Six

The passing of Mary Dearlove was marked, as it is in most civilized societies, by a funeral that reflected the former existence of a relatively prominent citizen. The Mayor spoke. Senior police officials attended, plus all the ARW's and most of the prominent families of Fort York. A Baptist minister eulogized Mary Dearlove. He went on at length about the tragic accident, the waste of it, how she would be missed, and dwelt exclusively on her positive qualities, avoiding the official demon rum theory that most people downplayed anyway.

By the end of March, the event had been pushed into the back of people's minds by the business of living and the war. It was impossible, and unpatriotic, to forget the conflict, but diversions were necessary. People enjoyed romance on the "Lux Radio Theatre" or" Ma Perkins". They laughed at Fibber McGee and Molly and shared in the "Adventures of the Falcon".

On the silver screen, Red Skelton clowned for everyone in *I Dood It*. People wept at *My Friend Flicka* or sat through desperate attempts at escapism like *Mexican Spitfire's Elephant* with Lupe Velez.

People were reading *A Tree Grows in Brooklyn*, *The Human Comedy* or Lloyd C. Douglas's *The Robe*. For lighter fare there was always "Popeye the Sailor", "Moon Mullins" or "The Gumps" in the comic section of the local newspaper. And some found temporary respite in the humour of everyday news items. But you had to search for them.

"I found one." Jake was reading a section of the *FY Expositor*, April fourteenth. He was in the kitchen with Tretheway and Beezul, who was staying for supper. They each had a part of the paper. Addie bustled about preparing the meal.

"'Large Gold Painted Cow's Head Stolen from East End Butcher Shop'." Jake looked up, smiling. "How's that?"

"Not bad," Tretheway nodded.

"What on earth will they do with it?" Addie asked.

"Here's another." Beezul read the headline. "'Shell from British Warship Lands in Boston Graveyard'."

"On purpose?" Jake grinned.

"No,no." Beezul read on. "Apparently they were cleaning the gun."

"And nobody knew it was loaded," Jake chuckled. Even Addie Smiled.

"Here's one," Tretheway said. "And this is funny. 'Man Cranks Car. Car Starts and Runs Over Him'."

Oh Albert," Addie said.

Jake and Beezul laughed.

"He wasn't hurt, Addie."

"I've got one close to home," Jake said. "'Thieves Grab Bag of Hair'."

"Close to home?" Tretheway asked.

"The barber shop in the hotel," Jake said.

"Frank's?"

"That's right.

"I was in there yesterday," Beezul said.

"Read on," Tretheway said.

"It says," Jake ran his fingers over the lines of type, "there were two bags. One the day's receipts. One the sweepings. Someone broke in and, I guess, stole the wrong bag."

"With the hair?" Tretheway asked.

Jake nodded.

"I'll bet they were surprised when they got it home." Addie said.

"I think I've got the winner," Beezul announced. He smoothed the paper out in front of him on the kitchen table. "'Set of Five Heavy Lawn Bowls Found In Stomach of Cow'."

"Good Lord," Addie said.

"But how could a cow. . ." Jake began.

"That's what it says," Beezul said.

"How did they find them?" Addie asked.

"You don't want to know," Beezul said.

Addie didn't press her point.

"That's the winner then." Tretheway folded up his section.

Beezul smiled as he collected the pieces of paper and took them into the family room. Addie disappeared downstairs to the root cellar for more spuds. Tretheway gazed out the back window. The snow had all melted away. There was a hint of gold in the willow trees and the grass was greener now than it had been a week ago. A black crow swaggered across the flagstone path cawing raucously.

"Something bothering you?" Jake asked his boss.

"The barber shop item," Tretheway said. "Doesn't sit right."

"Why not?"

"The two bags. They'd feel different. Why wouldn't they look inside? And take the right one?"

Jake thought for a moment. "Then it wouldn't be funny."

"You're right." Tretheway smiled. "Not as funny as the lawn bowls." He stood up and headed for the ice box.

Chapter Seven

An incident occurred on Thursday, May thirteenth, that definitely steered the thoughts of the Fort York populace away from the war. Unlike the radio shows or movies, the incident was not funny.

A beat constable discovered Squire Middleton at dawn in the centre of the city's main downtown intersection, King and James. He lay flat on his back, quite dead. According to the *FY Expositor*, "His outstretched arms and legs formed (if you included his head as the fifth point) a crude but obvious pentacle. In each clutching hand rested a pop-eyed owl. Both had been squeezed to death in the last paroxysms of a dying man. The horrible expression on the decease's face matched that of Mary Dearlove and her grinning gargoyle companions of mid-March. And both mysterious deaths occurred on the thirteenth of the month."

Beneath the Expo's purple prose lay a basic truth: Squire Middleton was dead; had been found in most unusual circumstances, at dawn, on the thirteenth, with the dead owls. No one could argue against these facts. But people began to believe conjecture. Rumours flooded the city. Mass hysteria was fueled by tales of everything from satanic Nazi paratroopers to extraterrestrial beings. Everyone had a wild theory—or almost everyone.

"I can't swallow it." Tretheway sat in his office with Jake, Beezul and Zoë Plunkitt. Wan Ho had provoked the impromptu meeting when he had walked in to bring them up to date. It was late afternoon, Friday.

"Can't swallow what?" Jake said.

"The mumbo jumbo. The owls. The pentacle. The whole witchcraft thing. It just doesn't fit in with the Squire." Tretheway looked at Wan Ho. "Do you know the cause of death yet?"

"Heart attack," Wan Ho answered. "Doc Nooner says it could've been caused by fright. Zulp suggested some sort of ceremony. Or ritual."

"At King and James?"

Wan Ho shrugged.

"How'd he get there?"

"We're working on it. There's a blank from eleven to dawn. We don't know where he was."

"Where was he at eleven?"

"Finishing his shift." Wan Ho explained. "At eleven o'clock, the Squire presumably locked up his street car. At the west end of the line. The loop. Then walked home. But he never arrived."

"Who saw him?"

Wan Ho consulted his notebook. "A police cruiser. At ten-fifty-five. They waved at each other. That would be just before he parked his street car."

"And after that?"

"No one." Wan Ho checked his book again. "At five-thirty a.m. the day conductor opened up the car. It was empty. Nothing amiss. He drove it right through the city. Eventually to the east end. About five miles."

"Past King and James?"

"Yes."

"What time?"

"Just before the sun came up."

"And you say," Tretheway persisted, "still nothing amiss?"

"Correct. He picked up some early shift workers at different stops, but saw nothing unusual along the way.

Even at King and James."

"There must be something else."

"What about his bag?" Jake asked. "The old school bag he kept his stuff in?"

"I'm coming to that," Wan Ho said defensively. "A passerby found it. At the end of the McKittrick Bridge curve. On the sidewalk. At first light."

"That's about a mile before King and James?"

"That's right," Wan Ho said. "Still on the streetcar line."

Tretheway ran out of questions.

"What now?" Jake asked.

"As Inspector Renault said in *Casablanca*, "Round up the usual suspects'." Wan Ho looked tired.

"And who might that be?" Zoë Plunkitt said, with a smile.

"You're not going to like this."

"Eh?"

"Zulp has a new theory." Wan Ho had their attention. "One of the Air Raid Wardens is a spy. A Nazi. He or she is knocking off the other ARW's. A plot against the Canadian Civil Defense. Starting in Fort York."

"You can't be serious," Tretheway said.

"He's outdone himself," Jake said.

Zoë was speechless.

"I said you wouldn't like it."

"Surely you don't believe it," Tretheway said.

"The Nazi spy thing, no. But in fairness to Zulp, Mary Dearlove and the Squire *were* ARW's."

"But so am I," Beezul said.

"Me too," Zoë said.

"So tell me where you were Wednesday night," Wan Ho said; then more softly, "just for the record."

"You asked the others?" Jake said.

"Yep. Garth Dingle, Gum, Pat Sprong, Cynthia, Tremaine. Even Doc Nooner."

"And?" Tretheway said.

"They all say they were in bed," Wan Ho said. "And can't prove it."

"You didn't ask me," Beezul said.

"Okay. Where were you?"

Beezul smiled sheepishly. "In bed."

"Anybody see you?"

He shook his head.

"Join the club."

"What about me?" Zoë Plunkitt asked.

"You were away," Wan Ho.said.

"You know?" Zoë went pale. "And I suppose you know where I went?"

"It doesn't matter. I know you weren't here."

"I was in New England. I always go there." Her lips pressed tightly together. "A town called Danvers."

"Take it easy, Zoë" Wan Ho said soothingly. "Look at it this way. You're the only one with an iron-clad alibi."

"Well. . ." The colour returned to her cheeks.

"I suppose you checked on Jake?" Tretheway said.

"No. Of course not."

"And me?"

Wan Ho hesitated. "Not really, but. . ."

"But what?"

"You know what Chief Zulp's like. He thinks you shouldn't dabble in. . ."

"I don't dabble," Tretheway said quietly.

"Poor choice of words." Wan Ho tugged at his collar which was suddenly too tight. "You know what I mean." He tried again. "He says you're the Regional ARP Officer, and doing a fine job. But you're not a detective. And he thinks you should. . .you know. . ."

"Stay the hell out of the investigation," Tretheway finished.

"Well, not in those exact words."

"Couldn't agree more," Tretheway said.

"Eh?"

"I have enough to do with my own job." He spread his arms and looked around. "Right here. And I certainly wouldn't want to interfere with the Chief's investigation."

Everyone relaxed.

"However." Tretheway stood up. Everyone stopped relaxing. Tretheway shook his fat forefinger at no one in particular. His eyes flashed. "As a senior officer of the FYPD, I have a responsibility to the people. If I deem there's an emergency, I'll do all the dabbling I want. Murder tends to erase the lines between detectives and traffic cops."

His great fist banged the desk. Pencils, paper clips and a framed picture of Tretheway's old traffic division jumped up about an inch from the solid oak table top. "A Third Class inside desk Constable can—hell, *must* arrest a killer!"

Wan Ho and Jake held their breath. Beezul hitched his pants up. Zoë Plunkitt stared intently into her lap. Tretheway sat down and began to realign his pencils.

"What's the time?"

"Eleven twenty," Jake said.

"Close enough." Tretheway stood up. "Let's have some fish and chips," he said. "My treat."

For the rest of the month, the investigation followed trails that dead-ended, criss-crossed, went in circles or just petered out. Zulp's large unwieldy unit (not including Tretheway) didn't lack energy. Their motto —'No Stone Unturned'—was repeated every morning by Zulp at the daily pep talk. Some upturned stones proved interesting, some amusing, but most were unnecessary. Negligible new evidence came to light.

By the beginning of June, the investigation had bogged down. Very little had changed. The Mary Dearlove case was still officially an accident but viewed now with suspicion. Luke had returned to the hotel on a trial basis but still couldn't, or wouldn't, remember anything about his grisly sighting. And the Squire's demise remained on the books as a killing by strange unknowns. This too was being questioned.

The June thirteenth murder shattered this air of indecision.

It was no accident. And it was obviously premeditated.

Chapter Eight

Early in the eighteenth century, Geoffrey Beezul's ancestors had left the US for Canada as part of the United Empire Loyalist movement. Since 1843, the year the Fort York Yacht Club received its Royal charter, a Beezul had been a member. Geoffrey carried on the tradition, this year as Rear-Commodore. Although his appointment had more to do with keeping the club's gin cupboard stocked than with seamanship, he did own and skipper a small Rainbow Class sailboat.

The pretty, 21-foot white craft, with keel and Marconi rig, called for a racing crew of three: Skipper Beezul, Mainman Warbucks and Jibman—in this case Jibwoman—Zoë Plunkitt. During the races Beezul was an inept sailor and Warbucks daydreamed but Zoë, the only active female member in the club, crewed with agility and knowledge, and did her best to keep them from coming in last—which they did often. They raced only once a week except for special occasions, like regattas.

The RFYYC had decided to host the Great Lakes International Regatta to celebrate its centennial on the weekend of June 12-13. On Saturday, ideal weather prevailed. The wind blew a reliable twenty knots, the sun shone and the temperature steadied around eighty degrees.

On the club's verdant bayside lawn, waiters circulated among the casually arranged tables and chairs, balancing pink lemonade and gins on gleaming silver trays. Ladies wearing flowered summer dresses walked arm in arm with men in white ducks and crested navy blazers. Local politicians, including the Mayor himself, hobnobbed with the officers of the club. Rear-Commodore Beezul had invited all the west-end ARWs, the Tretheways and Jake. Tretheway's blazer pocket displayed the splendid crest of the Second Life Guards, Household Cavalry.

Everyone jostled pleasantly for a view of the starting line. They waited expectantly to see the puff of smoke from the Committee boat and, seconds later, hear the small cannon's roar that signalled the start of the first race.

Lightnings, an international class, made up the largest group and started first. They were followed by small Snipes and smaller Penguins. Those with homemade, unique or scarce models fitted into an untidy miscellaneous class. Beezul raced in the last group against eight other Rainbows.

From the first starting cannon to the last finishing bell, all races went off without a hitch. And Skipper Beezul did better than anyone expected. Because of bad decisions by half the fleet, fluky wind shifts and just being in the right place at the right time, he finished second, a personal best.

This pleased Beezul immensely. He couldn't wait for the Sunday race. That night, as he slid into a dream in which he held the winner's cup above his head amongst his cheering peers, a small, nagging thought nibbled at the edge of his enjoyment: "If only the weather holds."

The barometer dropped alarmingly overnight. By Sunday morning the wind was gusting to forty knots, no sun appeared, the temperature had dipped to the high forties and uncomfortable darts of rain were falling erratically. Only the hardiest spectators turned up. The ladies had exchanged their floppy summer hats for bandannas.

Woollen sweaters and squall jackets were popular. Topsiders replaced dress shoes. Everyone kept turning a weather eye to the grey lowering skies.

"Doesn't look good." Beezul stared skyward from the dock. He had called an emergency pre-race meeting with his crew. The Rainbow rocked alongside.

"Maybe they'll call it off," Warbucks said hopefully.

"Surely they will." Beezul shared his mainman's hope.

Zoë said nothing.

In the past, when the weather changed suddenly for the worse—not unusual on the inland lakes of Fort York—Beezul simply didn't race. He would spend the afternoon in the card room with warm friends and gin. But this was different.

"Let's just go inside," Beezul suggested.

"Good idea," Warbucks said.

"We have to race," Zoë said.

"What?"

"Why?"

"Everyone expects us to," Zoë said. "We're in second place."

"But look at the weather," Beezul said, sulking.

"They've got to call it off," Warbucks said.

The sound of the fifteen-minute-warning cannon dashed the hopes of the two mariners.

"Let's go." Zoë jumped on board. "Where's my storm jib?"

Warbucks reluctantly maneuvered his boat out of the slip while Zoë snapped on the smaller jib and Warbucks roller-reefed the mainsail to a point where it was hardly worth raising.

"Tremaine," Zoë complained, "it's too small. We won't move at all."

"We're going about five knots now on the rigging," Warbucks said.

"I don't care," Zoë said. "It looks dumb."

"Raise it a little." Beezul's voice wavered. "We're getting close to the start."

Warbucks complied. The main now carried almost the same sail area as the set jib. Their speed increased. The Rainbow shot across the starting line, which bisected the bottom windward leg of the course triangle, at the same time the cannon roared. It was as though they'd planned it. Zoë cheered. Beezul smiled. Warbucks didn't hear it.

Beezul and crew tacked wildly back and forth toward the first marker. Three of the Rainbow fleet, racing with sails boldly unreefed, swamped. By the time Beezul somehow rounded the first buoy, there were only six boats left in the fleet, five ahead of him. On the next leg, a straight run before the wet, blasting north wind, two more dropped out with broken whisker poles and torn sails. The remaining four boats, Beezul trailing, rounded the second buoy to a choppy, exciting but relatively safe reach on their way to the last leg. The front runner, Saturday's winner, expertly rounded the final marker onto the windward leg once again. Numbers two and three weren't as expert. Reefed but still with too much sail, they also swamped. Minutes later Beezul passed them dead in the water.

Rear-Commodore Beezul looked ahead, past the heaving bow, bucking madly to windward with the boat at a forty-five degree angle. The one remaining Rainbow's stern showed an insurmountable five-minute lead. But he came next, second, a peak in his sailing career. It crossed Beezul's mind that his next successful race could be the Nationals or even the Olympics. He smiled and looked towards the shore. I wonder if anyone's watching, he thought.

Jake stood on the roof of the large lockers with Gum supporting him in the wind. For the last hour, he had been following the Rainbow race through an ancient telescope commandeered from the miniature RFYYC museum and shouting interim reports to the small crowd below on the dock.

"Can you see him?" Tretheway shouted.

"He's second," Jake shouted back. "A shoo-in for second."

Everyone cheered. Tretheway, Addie and the rest of Beezul's guests clustered around the *Rainbow*'s empty slip in front of his locker.

As the Rear-Commodore, Beezul rated a large, walk-in locker. The overhead garage door was open, allowing the guests to come in out of the rain and mingle freely amongst the untidy sailing bric-a-brac: half-empty, antifouling paint cans, sandpaper, extra sails, souvenir burgees from visiting yacht clubs, empty gin and vermouth bottles. A clutter of tools lay on the counter next to a dusty wind-up Victrola. Lined up neatly on a hundred-pound cake of ice stood a row of milk bottles filled with a deep purple liquid—Beezul's famous Bangers. Tretheway remembered later that one bottle had a piece of string tied loosely around its neck.

"Something's happening," Jake shouted.

Everyone ran out onto the dock.

"What?" Tretheway shouted.

"I can't see the first boat."

"What about Beezul?"

Jake squinted through the glass. "I see him. He's the only one left."

No one was more surprised than Beezul. He watched with amazement as the sails on the leading *Rainbow* disappeared, and the loud snap of the breaking mast carried back to him on the gale force wind.

"My God." Beezul realized they were first.

After two more tacks they sailed close to the dismasted *Rainbow*. The disconsolate crew sat, oblivious to the high wind and rain, staring at the stump of a spar. They didn't look up or wave as Beezul passed.

"Ready about!" Beezul pushed the tiller hard over. "Hard a lee!"

The *Rainbow*'s hull flattened out, turned nimbly through the eye of the wind, then back to a forty-five degree slant in the opposite direction onto what Beezul and crew hoped would be the last tack. They ducked under the boom and clambered up to hike on the other side.

From his position on the wet topsides, Beezul peered through the pattern of sails and shrouds over the pointed bow of the *Rainbow* to the committee boat now not too far away.

"I think we're going to do it," Beezul said.

"Of course we are," Zoë shouted.

A sudden shift of wind blew spray in their faces. Warbucks smiled the way he thought an old salt would smile and gave the main sheet one last, contemptuous and unnecessary yank. The pulley on the floorboards of the boat gave way completely. What had been, seconds before, a taut main sheet, became a loose snake of manila rope with ten feet of slack. Warbucks shot overboard like a flare from a Very pistol.

Zoë screamed. Beezul froze. They both watched while Warbucks landed in the choppy waters with a splash that was hardly noticeable in the storm. He swung around, still clutching the line now taut to the boom pulley, until he dragged directly astern, adding another white line to the wake. The *Rainbow* lost surprisingly little speed.

"Stop!" Zoë screamed. "We have to pick him up!"

Beezul tore his gaze away from the hapless mainman to the finish line only fifty yards distant. He checked Warbucks again.

"Hang on, Tremaine!" Beezul held his course. "We're almost there."

Zoë's protests were lost in the wind.

Seconds later, which seemed longer to the three of them—especially Warbucks—the bell rang to signal the first one over the finish line; and this time, the only one. Immediately Beezul turned into the wind. The boat flattened out and came to rest. They hauled Warbucks in. He was stunned but unharmed.

"Are we finished?" Warbucks's eyes were glassy.

They lowered the mainsail and reset the jib. Beezul steered toward shore while Zoë helped Warbucks unclench his stiff fingers from around the sodden main sheet.

The mood on shore was jubilant. There had been a momentary concern when Jake reported Warbucks's sudden plunge over the side. But when the pealing bell signalled the winner and Warbucks was hauled back on board, Jake and Gum danced on the roof, hugging each other.

The victorious *Rainbow* entered the protection of the Yacht Club's basin to the cheers and happy shouts of the hardy spectators. Beezul couldn't stop smiling. His crew smiled too, although Warbucks's eyes were still glazed. As jibman, Zoë fended off the boat's prow from the dock, then made ready to jump ashore and tie up. Warbucks unchivalrously grabbed Zoë by the collar and pulled her back into the cockpit. He jumped ahead of her onto the dock.

"A Banger!" Warbucks pushed between Garth Dingle and Patricia Sprong, but ran around Tretheway into the locker. "I'm in dire need of a Banger!"

The Beezul Banger tradition had started in a small way about ten years before. After a particularly late finish in a club race, Beezul felt a quick lift was called for for himself and his crew. The ingredients were chosen simply because they were there. A syrupy dark rum from the Islands formed fifty percent of the base. To this was added strong prune juice, a dash of soda water and a liberal shake of Tabasco sauce. A fresh green onion was stirred in with the elements in a large tumbler and remained as an ornament. "They should be served cold, but no ice," Beezul always said. "No dilution." And as everyone knew, Beezul was his own best customer. Tretheway for one, could not understand the popularity of Beezul Bangers among club members. But as Jake pointed out, "The price is right."

Cynthia Moon and Addie were rinsing out dusty glasses at the sink when Warbucks barged in. They watched as he seized one of the milk bottles filled with the inky liquid, tore off the elastic and temporary cellophane top and took several large swigs. He wiped his mouth with the back of his hand and stared at Cynthia and Addie.

"Does that ever hit the spot!" Two purple rivulets ran from the corner of Warbucks's mouth into his grey beard, but his eyes had lost their glassiness.

Zoë caught up to him. 'Put that down."

"Pardon?"

"You're drinking too fast. And out of the bottle."

"She's right, Tremaine." Addie handed Warbucks a clean glass.

"Oh, no you don't." Warbucks said; he hugged the milk bottle to his chest.

"Let me have it," Zoë said. "You should get into something dry."

"Leave him alone." Beezul came up to them. "A Banger'll dry out anyone." He reached for another milk bottle. Cynthia handed him a glass. Zoë took one too.

"A toast to the winning crew." Warbucks raised his bottle high, and took another deep swig.

"Here, here." Beezul raised his glass. So did Zoë, reluctantly. Others joined in. Beezul Bangers were passed around. Someone put a record on the Victrola. Warbucks started dancing by himself. Beezul danced with anyone near him. Garth's, Pat Sprong's, Cynthia's, Wan Ho's, Jake's and even Addie's lips showed the tell-tale purple of the Banger drinker. Tretheway and Doc Nooner stood off to one side sipping Scotch.

"Good party," Doc Nooner said.

"If he's any indication, yes." Tretheway huddled toward Warbucks who was laughing loudly and spinning around by himself.

"He won a race, don't forget."

"So did Beezul and Zoë. You don't see them imitating a whirling dervish."

"They also haven't had a quart of Bangers."

"You're right." Tretheway smiled.

Warbucks stopped spinning while the music continued.

"C'mon. Join the party." He waved toward Tretheway.

"We're okay, Tremaine," Tretheway answered.

"Not you. The people behind you."

Tretheway and Doc automatically turned around. No one was there. The record finished. Warbucks started spinning again. "Love that piece."

"What was that all about?" Tretheway looked at Doc. Doc raised his eyebrows. "I don't know."

The temperature and humidity in the locker room were increased by the natural heat of wet-clothed bodies pressed together imbibing and dancing. People spilled out into the late dull afternoon. Despite the persistent cool showers, their mood remained exuberant.

It dropped temporarily when word arrived of a protest by the dismasted skipper under the rule which dictated that "The same number of crew members must finish the race as started the race." But this was disallowed by the racing committee with the decision that although Warbucks was ten yards behind the boat, he was still physically attached by the main sheet and therefore technically still part of the crew. It was official. Beezul had won the Rainbow

Division.

Beezul's smile broadened. Even Zoë's purple lips turned up. But Warbucks seemed to be out of it.

"Albert." Addie and Cynthia Moon approached Tretheway. You'd better talk to Tremaine."

"Why?"

"He's out on the lawn. Crying."

"More like sobbing," Cynthia said.

Tretheway sighed "You'd better come with me, Doc."

They found Warbucks standing close to the water, gazing out across the grey expanse of Fort York Harbour. He had stopped crying, but damp marks streaked the purple parts of his face.

"How's it going, Tremaine?" Tretheway asked.

"I just saw Mother." His gaze remained on the harbour.

"Eh?"

"Where?" Doc Nooner asked.

"Out there." Warbucks pointed to the open water. "She was in a dinghy. Coming toward me. My dog was with her."

"Your mother died," Tretheway said gently. "Ten, fifteen years ago."

"So did your dog," Doc said.

"Henley. A King Charles spaniel."

"Tremaine," Tretheway put his hand on Warbucks's shoulder, "There's no one there."

Warbucks bolted. Tretheway and Doc were taken unaware but gave chase. Some members, thinking it was part of the fun and games, joined the hunt. Warbucks led them across the rain-soaked lawn, between empty chairs and tables, scattering sea gulls and pigeons and constantly repeating "Henley, Henley." The chase ended when Warbucks slipped and fell going up a terrace of wet grass. Doc Nooner was the first to kneel beside him. Warbucks lay flat on his back, eyes wide open, pupils huge, staring heedless into the falling rain.

"There's more here than too much booze." Tretheway leaned over the two.

Doc Nooner nodded. He put the palm of his hand on Warbucks's rapidly rising and falling chest. "I don't like the way he's breathing."

Tretheway straightened up. He caught Jake's eye on the edge of the crowd. "Ambulance!" he shouted.

The sober command stilled the Henley chant that someone had started. Someone opened an umbrella over Warbucks. Several offers of help came from the crowd.

By the time the ambulance came, most of the people who had been outside had joined the regatta celebration continuing in the main clubhouse. Few of them knew about the events on the front lawn. Those who had joined in the chase thought it was simply the result of overindulgence. Only Tretheway and Doc were aware that Warbucks might be in serious trouble. And, Tretheway thought darkly to himself, maybe one other.

Doc Nooner volunteered to go in the ambulance with Warbucks to the hospital while Tretheway went back to the clubhouse. Beezul had pushed several tables together at the back of the room; he and his guests sat awaiting the prize presentations. They were all concerned about Warbucks, but not alarmed.

"I mean," Garth said, "these things happen. The race. The excitement. And all those fast Bangers."

A party atmosphere prevailed. People changed to other alcoholic beverages when the Bangers ran out. Tretheway switched from Scotch to Blue. He had just ordered a quart when the call came. He answered the phone.

"Tretheway."

"Nooner here. It's about Warbucks."

"Go on."

"He just passed away."

"Good Lord!"

"We don't know why. Won't know till the autopsy. But..." Doc Nooner hesitated again. "Keep it to yourself. It has all the earmarks of a poison. Some sort of hallucinatory drug. One that eventually leads to paralysis. He just stopped breathing."

"Poor bugger."

"You'll have to tell everybody there."

"I know." Tretheway grimaced.

When he got back to the table, a fresh Molson's Blue sat at his place. At the front of the room, the Commodore of the RFYYC was presenting Beezul with his first place, engraved trophy—"Winner, Rainbow Class, 1943, Great Lakes Regatta." A congratulatory message crackled over the PA system. Everyone cheered, except Tretheway.

Beezul marched back to his table holding the trophy on high. "C'mon everyone!" he shouted, "To the hospital!"

"Hold it a minute, Beezul." Tretheway raised both hands in the air to silence the crowd. It had little effect. "We can't go."

"Sure we can. We have to show Tremaine. Couldn't've done it without him."

"Listen, everybody!" Tretheway slapped the table, disturbing the glasses and ash trays. This time people stopped talking. "I've got some bad news." He looked right at Beezul. "I'm sorry. Warbucks is dead."

Beezul finally stopped smiling.

Although most of the celebrants wouldn't hear about the Warbucks tragedy until the next day, the party wound down quickly after the trophies were awarded. Beezul went home, forgetting his cup. Garth and Gum disconsolately walked the grounds together. Wan Ho had gone to the hospital. Addie, Pat Sprong, Cynthia and Zoë were, Tretheway thought, visiting the ladies' room.

Only Tretheway and Jake still sat at the table. Tretheway wrestled inwardly with his half promise to Doc Nooner. He wanted to confide in Jake.

"Poison?" Jake said.

"Keep it down," Tretheway cautioned. "We're not sure."

"How?" Jake lowered his voice.

"Probably in the Bangers."

"He had enough of those."

"And they'd cover the taste of anything."

"Just a minute," Jake said. "Everybody had Bangers."

"Warbucks drank from one bottle only. Remember?"

"So only one was poisoned?"

Tretheway nodded.

"Then how did anyone know. . ."

"It was marked," Tretheway remembered. "A piece of string." He stood up. "It might behoove us to slip over to the locker. Check the bottles."

"Good," Jake said. "We can join the ladies."

"What?"

"Addie, Cynthia, Zoë and. . ."

"What are they doing there?"

"Cleaning up. You know Addie. Beezul's gone home and they thought. . ."

"Christ!" Tretheway pushed tables and chairs aside getting to the door, Jake following closely. They ran across the lawn around the corner of the dock to the locker.

"What are you doing?" Tretheway said more loudly and harshly than he had intended.

The four women stopped what they were doing.

"We're cleaning up," Zoë said.

"Shouldn't we?" Addie frowned at her brother.

Tretheway's eyes swept the room. Addie was putting away glasses. Zoë's arms were up to her elbows in soapy water. Pat Sprong and Cynthia held damp towels. Then

Tretheway saw the milk bottles, all of them sitting on the counter, no purple stains, as clean and sparkling as when they were new. And not one had a string around its neck.

"Certainly," Tretheway lied. "Good idea."

"We just came over to see if we could help," Jake said.

"No, thanks." Cynthia smiled at him.

"We're just about finished," Pat Sprong said.

Addie regarded the two in suspicious silence.

Tretheway and Jake left quietly.

"What now?" Jake asked.

"Wait for the autopsy," Tretheway said, shrugging.

"Atropa Belladonna." Doc Nooner read from his open file folder. "Common name, deadly nightshade. Produces symptoms of extreme exuberance at first, then hallucinations, delirium, respiratory problems and eventually paralysis. Warbucks was full of it."

Jake winced at Doc Nooner's clinical choice of words. "But why? What's the motive?"

"We don't know," Wan Ho said. "Random. Occult. Just crazy. Take your pick. I don't know why the Squire was killed either." He threw his hands up. "Or if both deaths connected."

"Let me finish. It might help." Doc Nooner went back to his file. "Nightshade grows wild in Eastern U. S. and, I'm sure, here. Tall, ugly perennial herb. A leafy bush with flowers that turn into black berries. Filled with a sweet, violet juice. Probably looks like Bangers."

"Why the botany lesson?" Tretheway asked. "Who cares what the plant looks like?"

"The samples we took from Warbucks weren't chemically pure," Doc explained.

"What's that mean?" Wan Ho asked.

"It means that whoever did the deed, didn't walk into a drug store and buy it. It was full of impurities. In short, home-made."

"You mean someone found a bush somewhere?" Wan Ho asked.

"Or grew it."

The room fell silent. Tretheway reached for a cigar. Wan Ho stood up and began to pace—not really practical behavior in the Tretheway's small parlour where the four of them were meeting. Jake poked Fat Rollo to stop his snoring.

Tretheway broke the silence. "You mean that out there somewhere," he waved his arm, spraying cigar ash around, "we've got a witch's garden?"

Doc Nooner shrugged.

"And Zulp has all these facts?"

Wan Ho nodded.

"So I guess everybody's looking for bushes?"

"Optometrists."

"Eh?"

"Belladonna's the drug an eye doctor puts in your eyes before an examination," Wan Ho explained.

"That's right," Doc Nooner confirmed. "Dilates the pupils."

"And you bump into things for about an hour after," Jake added.

Doc nodded.

"So the usual suspects in this case," Wan Ho went on, "are optometrists, opticians, ophthalmologists. Even druggists. Especially those who are members of the Yacht Club, Zulp says."

"I don't believe it," Tretheway said.

"Do you think that's the way to go?" Jake asked Wan Ho.

"I follow orders. But on the inside," Wan Ho smiled, "it's known as 'The Evil League of Optometry Caper'."

Everyone chuckled.

By the end of June, the investigation had made little progress. Warbucks had been poisoned with a massive dose of belladonna by person or persons unknown. The poison had been presumably mixed with Beezul's over-powering Bangers in one of the milk bottles from the locker. All evidence had been efficiently removed from the bottles by Addie and her zealous friends. Prominent members of the RFYYC and the optical industry had been questioned at length; dispensing pharmacists had been queried. All in vain.

Even the search for ugly green bushes with bell-shaped flowers and black berries had been abandoned, not because they couldn't be found, but because there were too many. Some were growing in the special herb section of the FY Royal Botanical gardens, some were cultivated by local garden societies. A few flourished wild in secluded areas of Coote's Paradise. Cynthia Moon told Tretheway that one was blooming in her own private garden. She confessed to using small portions of the juice occasionally for makeup. And if a bit ran into her eyes, she didn't worry: "it makes them sparkle," she said.

All in all, it was a bad time for Chief Zulp. The Toronto newspapers criticized him and his detectives for the meagre results unearthed by their investigation. Even the local *FY Expositor* faulted Zulp's handling of the Warbucks poisoning. And it kept posing questions. 'Where was Squire Middleton from midnight to dawn on his fateful day?' 'What really happened to Mary Dearlove?' In a short editorial, the *Expo* strongly suggested that her spectacular fall may just possibly not have been an accident.

Zulp bristled at this criticism from his hometown paper. He brashly announced that he had secret information: a practical plan to bring 'an end to these heinous crimes'. When pressed for more information by the newsmen, he drew himself up, squeezed his eyes almost shut, adding more creases to his already creased face, and answered cryptically, "Knowledge is power."

Zulp's powerful knowledge was born of desperation. All he had was what everyone else had—the number thirteen. The murders and other strange, unsettling events had happened on, or close to, the thirteenth of each month. In researching the months of 1943, he had stumbled across the April 13 newspaper article about the five large bowls found in the cow's stomach. He found this sufficiently significant to dispatch two of his more toadying detectives to the Village of Fruitland where it had happened. When they left the farm none the wiser, the farmer, no friend of the police, phoned the *FY Expositor*. The result was another insulting news story.

Zulp reacted impulsively again. He insisted there was a definite connection between the murders and the bizarre incident.

"And furthermore," Zulp went on, "I can promise the people of Fort York that no murders, strange happenings or mysterious deaths will occur on the next thirteenth." He checked his calendar. "That's July thirteenth. A Tuesday. Or I will resign."

This raised eyebrows on the force, including Tretheway's.

"You don't suppose he knows something?"

Wan Ho shook his head. "All bluff."

"You mean something might happen in July?" Jake asked.

"All we can do is hope," Tretheway quipped.

As luck would have it, Zulp didn't have to step down in July.

Chapter Nine

It was the time of the year when the Dog Star rose and set with the sun, giving its name to the hot, uncomfortable days of summer. More than once, violent thunderstorms with hail chased Jake and Garth, along with other members of WSGCC, off the golf course. And the balmy, golden interludes between disturbances seemed shorter this year.

Most of Tretheway's friends escaped the city's heat at one time or another. Beezul, as usual, spent the whole two months at his secluded island summer home on Lake Muskoka. Zoë charitably took the recuperating Luke with her to visit friends in Massachusetts. Gum and his mother stayed for a week in an old hotel overlooking Niagara Falls. Doc Nooner went off his diet again to attend a medical convention in Cleveland. Major Patricia Sprong travelled to Windsor/Detroit on Salvation Army business. Cynthia Moon and Addie took the train to Toronto several times for shopping trips, but most days, Cynthia said she just "lolled around her garden." Wan Ho took some days off that he had coming but he never really stopped thinking about his job.

By the time July had squandered its thirty-one days, the allies had landed in Sicily: a coup d'etat had occurred in Italy and the strutting Mussolini had been arrested, U.S. Liberators had bombed Java and Japanese troops had secretly evacuated Kiska in Alaska. But nothing of note happened in Fort York on the thirteenth. Zulp later restated his promise of resignation, if necessary, for August. His luck held.

The dog days of summer continued in August. In Fort York, everyone waited apprehensively while the thirteenth approached and heaved a collective sigh of relief, almost as loud as the July thirteenth sigh, when it passed harmlessly. Tretheway and Jake were no exception.

"A good day over," Jake said.

Tretheway nodded. "I wonder why, though."

"Maybe it's finished," Addie shouted from inside the kitchen. "Maybe there won't be any more..."

"Maybe you're right, Addie," Jake encouraged.

Tretheway shook his head without speaking. He and Jake were sipping tea on the back porch and enjoying the stillness of late evening; relief from another humid day. Fat Rollo jumped on a noisy cricket while Fred lay panting beside Jake, thankful for an occasional rub behind her ear. It was Saturday, August fourteenth.

"It's been two whole months," Jake continued. "Maybe nothing more will happen."

Tretheway shook his head again. "I don't think so."

Dishes rattled in the kitchen.

"There's too many whys." Tretheway lowered his voice. "Why Hickory Island? Why the rabbit's foot? Why Mary Dearlove? The Squire? Or Warbucks?" He put his big cup down and looked at Jake. "And now you just brought up the next why."

"Eh?"

"Why has it stopped? Why have the incidents or murders not continued? A logical chain of events broken. Why? Tell me why."

Jake thought for a moment. "Everybody needs a holiday?" He smiled weakly.

"That's the dumbest..."

"Everybody does need a holiday," Addie interrupted. she stood at the screen door drying her hands on a tea towel. "Even policemen," she said to her brother.

106

"Eh?"

"You know Beezul invited you to his cottage."

"True," Tretheway said.

"It'd do the two of you good to get away."

There was a bit of a lull, Tretheway thought. His desk was relatively clear. The war was going well, which lent less urgency to air raid precautions. And it was hot in the city.

"What do you think, Jake?"

"A little fishing, a little sun," Jake said thoughtfully.

"Peace and quiet," Addie said.

"Sounds good," Jake said.

"Well," said Tretheway. "Maybe a couple of days."

"That's settled, then." Addie folded up the tea towel. "You could leave next Saturday. Take the whole week." She checked the Toronto Maple Leaf wall calendar in the kitchen. "That's the twenty-first."

"Good idea." Tretheway pushed himself out of the sturdy garden chair. "I'll leave a message for Beezul."

They left the following Saturday. Jake had the top down on the '33 Pontiac and the rumble seat stuffed with luggage and Molson's Blue. The trip took eight hours. They got lost three times, had one flat tire and, during the last part of the journey into the Ontario northland, had to give a warning honk at every turn in the narrow road. When Jake finally turned the wheel of the black machine off at the main highway into the village of Beaumaris, they were still early. The weary travellers waited on the dock until the pre-arranged time. As there was no contact with the isolated island, all messages had to be phoned to the Beaumaris General Store well ahead of time, then relayed to Beezul directly whenever he made his trip to the mainland for supplies and mail. When he eventually putted up to the dock, smiling and waving in his outboard motor boat, Tretheway and Jake were very glad to see him. Beezul, however, had underestimated the mass of the two men — especially Tretheway — and their luggage. Two trips were necessary. Tretheway was forced to remain, red-faced, on the dock while Beezul made the half-hour round trip with Jake and the supplies — not a good beginning.

But the rest of the week, Tretheway and Jake both agreed later, was idyllic. They enjoyed seven days of vivid blue skies, fleecy scudding clouds, no rain and unbelievably clear and sparkling nights. Jake and Beezul fished casually while Tretheway lay on the dock giving — Beezul's neighbors said behind their hands — a realistic imitation of a dead white whale. The daily highlight was what Beezul called the "champagne cruise." It took about an hour, just before dinner. For this, they lovingly dusted the Ditchburn: a long, dark, mahogany needle-nosed craft with a gleaming deck you could comb your hair in. A relic of the luxurious twenties, the powerful inboard majestically carved the waters between the islands of Lake Muskoka allowing Tretheway and Jake, sitting in their individual wicker chairs behind Beezul, to raise their champagne-filled crystal flutes in a salute other Ditchburns doing the same thing.

"I could get used to this," Jake said.

Tretheway refilled his glass from the pewter ice bucket. "What are the poor people doing today?" he mused.

The evening meal followed. With Beezul concocting small delicious gourmet treats and Tretheway's knack for getting the most out of cooking simple fare, they ate well. Jake worried at different times about the extra weight he was sure they were all putting on, but said nothing. Beezul inveigled his housekeeper, Elsie, a grey-haired family retainer whose age no one, herself included, knew, to be the fourth at euchre. She proved a surprisingly good player. Her aces hit the card table every bit as aggressively as Tretheway's. Just before bed, they carried a Blue, wine, or Scotch outside for some lazy educational star gazing. The cycle began again the next day after an eye-opening dip. Seven days passed quickly.

Chapter Ten

Tretheway, Jake and—after Labour Day—Beezul, arrived back at their desks in a spirit of optimistic enthusiasm. They looked as good as they felt. Their complexions showed the flattering result of the sun, although Tretheway's was on the red side. The three were well prepared, they thought, to face whatever the devils of Fort York had in store for them in the fall season.

In September, Italy officially surrendered; the allies landed at Salerno; Australian and U.S. troops invaded New Guinea and Zulp, fortunately for him, did not renew his promise of resignation for the thirteenth of the month, a Monday. Tretheway got the call shortly after midnight.

"It's a fire," Wan Ho said. He sounded excited, or at least as excited as a Sergeant of Detectives ever gets.

"Do you know what time it is?" Tretheway asked.

"Sorry. I thought you'd want to know."

"About a fire?" Tretheway said.

Jake appeared beside Tretheway. "What's up?"

"Wan Ho's got a fire." Tretheway didn't bother to cover the mouthpiece.

"That's nice."

"Sorry," Wan Ho said again. "Perhaps I should explain."

"Good idea."

"About twenty minutes ago I got a phone call from the dispatcher at Central. A house mother at the University said two of her students noticed a glow just outside their

111

dormitory window. Turned out to be a large bonfire. About a hundred yards from the residence. Half hidden by some trees and small knolls. At the edge of the campus by the ravine. One or two people were spotted running away. You with me?"

"Go on," Tretheway said.

"The fire was deliberately set, albeit prematurely. It was supposed to be lit on the weekend. Some sort of initiation ceremony."

"End of Hell Week." Jake listened ear to ear with his boss as Tretheway bent over and held the receiver upright. "Freshman hazing," Jake remembered.

"It's still just a fire," Tretheway said into the mouthpiece.

"Pieces of wood, logs, old desks, combustibles of all kinds were piled around, for want of a better word, a stake. At its top, were the stake is exposed, maybe twenty feet above the ground, a person was tied. Securely."

Wan Ho paused. Neither Tretheway nor Jake spoke.

"It sounded like a woman, they said."

"Sounded?"

"She was singing."

"We'll meet you there."

Tretheway and Jake got there just ahead of Wan Ho. A soft, late summer drizzle had been falling since sundown. Closer to mist than rain, it had done little to impede the blaze. A large crowd made up mostly of resident students still huddled under their umbrellas around the smouldering pyre. The firemen had wetted down the bonfire enough to pull the unrecognizable body carefully from the smoking cinders. It rested now under a tarpaulin, waiting for Doc Nooner.

Jake held high a large striped golf umbrella he kept in the car. It covered him and most of Tretheway. They stood beside Wan Ho as he officially questioned the two witnesses. A house mother hovered in the background. Both the young coeds were wide-eyed first-year students fresh from the farm fields of Northern Ontario.

"I'll never forget it," the first girl said.

"Neither will I," the second one said.

"I understand you saw someone running away," Wan Ho began.

"That's right. Two of them."

"When we went out." The second girl nodded vigorously.

"Could you tell who? Man? Woman? Any idea of age?"

"No. Too dark."

"It was raining."

"Where did they go?" Wan Ho asked.

They both pointed over Wan Ho's shoulder to Chegwin, a nature trail behind the Science Building that led into the ravine.

"There."

"Down the woods."

"And the fire?" Wan Ho said.

"Just started."

"About halfway up the pile."

"It was supposed to be for a party Saturday."

"Some party now."

"And you mentioned singing?" Wan Ho asked.

"That's what I'll never forget."

"Me neither. At the top of her voice."

"Her?" Wan Ho asked. "You're sure it was a woman?"

"We could see better then. With the fire."

"She had a uniform on."

"Do you remember what she was singing?" Wan Ho asked.

"Every word."

"She sang it over and over."

The two of them started to chant. "'The devil and me, we don't agree. I hate him and he hates me.'"

Wan Ho looked at Tretheway and Jake.

"Then the singing stopped."

"The flames got higher."

"Then she screamed."

"She screamed forever."

"Okay," Wan Ho rested his hands on the girls' shoulders. "You've both been a big help."

Tretheway signalled the house mother. She put her arms around the girls and led them back to their dormitory.

The three men stood in the mist and stared mesmerized at the firemen sifting through the charred debris. Most of the students returned to their dry dorms. Two policemen in rain slickers patrolled the site.

"Well, there's not much doubt about it, is there?" Tretheway said.

Jake shook his head.

"Doesn't look like it," Wan Ho said.

"She was always singing that song," Jake said.

"I'd never heard all the words before," Wan Ho said.

"I had," Tretheway remembered. "I talked to her once about it. It was her favourite. A very old Salvation Army hymn."

"And then there's the uniform," Jake said.

"The clincher," Wan Ho confirmed.

When they heard the sirens and squealing of tires that heralded Zulp's arrival at the front of the building, Wan Ho left to report. Tretheway and Jake ducked into the shelter of one of the many covered Gothic archways that graced the campus. From its shadows, they watched as policemen darted through the drizzle and smoke into the woods at Zulp's raucous commands.

Doc Nooner found them. "Where's Wan Ho?"

"I imagine he's joined the search," Tretheway said.

"Oh?"

"An hour too late."

"In the rain," Jake said.

"Down trails that are unfamiliar," Tretheway added.

"In the dark," Jake added.

"I take it you two don't hold out much hope for the search?" Doc Nooner said.

"None whatsoever," Tretheway said.

"Did you find out anything, Doc?" Jake asked.

Nooner shook his head. "Pretty burnt up."

"No identification, then?" Tretheway asked.

"Nothing medical yet. Can't tell till later. The autopsy. Skin tissue. Teeth. Teeth can tell you a lot."

Jake winced. "For God's sake, Doc!"

"But you must have an idea," Tretheway persisted.

"Oh yes," Doc said. "Probably the same as you. The uniform. The singing. It pretty well has to be, or had to be, Patricia Sprong. . ."

They stared out at the darkened campus. A fresh wind rattled the ivy covering the rough grey walls.

"She was a nice lady." Tretheway puffed life into half a cigar.

"I liked her too." Jake glanced at his boss. "What now?"

"I think it's time we joined the fight."

"Eh?" Jake looked at Tretheway. So did Doc Nooner.

"It's time to stop the killings. Time to figure out who did it. And get him. Or her. In short, we must logically and sensibly proceed. Investigate."

"I thought you were supposed to stick to ARP work," Doc Nooner said.

"That's right," Jake started. "Zulp said. . ."

"I deem this an emergency. There's an immediacy here that overshadows waiting for incendiary bombs to fall at King and James. In the words of the Bard, 'necessity's sharp pinch' forces us to act."

Tretheway's cigar resembled a spinning fiery pinwheel as he flipped it into the wet night. "Let's go, Jake. There's lots to do."

Jake smiled—nervously, but still a smile.

Chapter Eleven

For the rest of the month, Tretheway was as good as his word. He found lots to do. Sometimes he included Jake, but most of the time, Jake just drove and dropped his boss off at seemingly haphazard spots of Tretheway's choosing. They visited Cynthia Moon, Wan Ho, Luke, the hotel, the RFY Botanical Gardens, the FY Street Railway car barns, the extensive morgue of the *FY Expositor*, the University, the Yacht Club, the barber shop, and it seemed to Jake that every other trip ended at the central library or one of its branches. All this time, Beezul, Zoë Plunkitt and, sometimes Jake, held down the ARP fort.

Tretheway spent his evenings alone in his quarters except for trips to restock his ice box. More than once, Jake or Addie asked if they could help or do anything, but Tretheway's polite, if monosyllabic answers, warned them away. They both—particularly Jake—knew from experience that Tretheway would bring them up to date when he was ready; that he would even insist on it. He was ready the first week in October.

"Jake. How'd you like to join me upstairs for some nut brown ale?" Tretheway phrased his invitation casually, so that it would not sound like a command. Jake knew better. But he was also eager to know what was going on.

"Love to." Jake nodded at Addie and some students as he and Tretheway passed through the kitchen. Jake followed his boss up the narrow back stairs, stopping at the dark oak door, now open, that separated Tretheway's domain from the rest of the house. Tretheway ushered him in. Jake was struck, as always, by the comfortable aura that surrounded him when he entered the bright, high-ceilinged room. The fireplace glowed with a small fire lit to fight a dip in the early fall temperature. A quiet ballad was playing on the radio. An untidy but homey pile of books and papers lay on Tretheway's roll-top desk. Photographic milestones and accomplishments from his uniformed past hung on the opposite wall. Fat Rollo didn't look so big on the huge bed. There was a pleasant mixture of the smells of shoe polish and cologne. In the centre of the room stood an out-of-place easel supporting a large manila pad.

Tretheway made immediately for the corner ice box, hidden discreetly by an exquisitely decorated Chinese screen (gift from Wan Ho). He popped two Blues.

"You want some cheese?" Tretheway asked.

"Sure."

Tretheway took a two-pound sliced wedge of four-year-old Canadian cheddar out of the ice box, and put it with some crackers on a side table close to Jake. He handed Jake his quart of beer, then drank half of his own from the bottle. Jake pulled a footstool up in front of the easel and made himself comfortable. He had been here before.

From the easel tray, Tretheway took a jumbo pencil with the words "Souvenir 1938 Canadian National Exhibition" emblazoned on its length and, without preamble, drew a large "W" on the pad.

"That's who we're after," he said.

"W?" Jake said.

"W for witch."

"A woman?"

"Not necessarily." Tretheway took a deep breath. "I've done a lot of research these past weeks. Most of it on witchcraft. There is a school that applies the word 'witch' to man or woman. Let's leave it at that. Let's not get into the differences between white witches, warlocks, wizards or sorcerers. It's too confusing. And you'll always get an argument."

"Okay with me." Jake pulled on his quart.

"And on witches, our W springs directly from black folklore. From the world of broomsticks coursing across night skies." Tretheway advanced slowly toward Jake. "From the world of demonic hares, strident spying crows, malevolent spiders, hemlock harvested at midnight, evil spells cast at crossroads, black cats that foretell bad weather, eye of newt, toe of frog, toad spittle."

By this time, Tretheway was bent over and only inches from Jake's face. Jake leaned away. The hackles rose on his neck and shoulders.

"Surely you're joking," Jake said.

Tretheway straightened up abruptly. "Jake. Where's your imagination? We have to get into the mind of an evil spirit. Think like a witch. Act like our W. But at the same time," he shook his big pencil in the air, "keep both our feet on the mortal, solid ground of law enforcement."

Jake felt slightly reassured. "Right."

"Now, through a combination of research, intuition, process of elimination, intelligent assumption and just straightforward common sense, I've put all the pieces of the puzzle together, or almost all, in one big logical picture."

Tretheway deliberately put a piece of cheese in his mouth and followed it with a cracker. Jake waited patiently while his boss chewed—longer than necessary, he thought.

"Assume one thing," Tretheway continued. "W had a plan. It went a little bit off track. But W had a definite scheme."

Jake looked a question.

"To do away with one person." Tretheway drew a numeral one on the pad beside W. "Only one."

"Do you know who?"

"Yes."

"Then. . ."

"Patience." Tretheway held his hand up as though Jake were a speeding truck. "Let's go back to the start. Remember?"

"Hickory Island?"

"That's right." Tretheway drew a line underneath W and the number one. He wrote in "Hickory Island, Jan. 13" and drew another line underneath. "W was alone. Probably drugged. Conducting a ceremony. One W obviously believed in. Incantation, black mass, reading from the devil's book. I don't know. It doesn't matter. You saw the symbols. The pentacles. The circle. Smelled the brimstone."

"And the number," Jake added.

"That's something else."

"Eh?"

"It didn't fit."

"What did it mean?"

"I don't know." Tretheway paused. "But it was important to W. And it was a date. The year 1692. But let's get back to Hickory Island. The melted wax. The bronze bowl. And pins. All part of image magic. W was probably sticking pins in our victim's effigy before melting it. And the witch's ladder. A perverted rosary. Also used in casting spells. Remember Cynthia's words? 'An impish presence bent on malevolence'." Tretheway shook his head. "Now I believe her. And W didn't expect company. This had been planned for the thirteenth. Don't forget the blackout was a surprise. No one would've noticed W's fire if all the lights had been on."

"And we scared W away," Jake said.

"To fight another day."

"Which would be Mary Dearlove," Jake frowned.

"Don't forget the rabbit."

"That's part of it?"

"Very much so." Tretheway scrawled "Rabbit's Foot, Feb. 13" on the manila pad. "W indoctrinated an assistant that night. A necessary helper. W needed an Ygor, a hunchback, a junior partner in sorcery. Preferably someone fiercely loyal, physically strong who W could easily dominate mentally."

"Luke?"

"Yes. W formed a bond with the impressionable Luke by having him take part in a midnight ritual. More incantations, I'm sure. And magic rabbit lore. There's no need going into whether the rabbit was dead or alive when they cut off its leg."

Jake winced.

"This incident is important because it led directly to the next one."

"Now Mary Dearlove."

Tretheway nodded.

"Was it murder then?"

"Yes."

Tretheway wrote, "Mar. 13, Mary Dearlove" on the pad under "Rabbit's Foot". He connected the two with an arrow.

"Mary Dearlove somehow connected the rabbit episode to Luke and—although she didn't know it at the time—W. Maybe she saw Luke with it. Maybe he bragged about it. Mary could be very charming when she was after a story."

Jake nodded.

"A meeting was arranged. Time and place, of course, chosen by W. Midnight. Roof Garden." Tretheway pointed the pencil at Jake. "You were there."

"At exactly twelve o'clock." Jake remembered the chimes.

"Not really," Tretheway contradicted. "I checked with

City Hall. The janitor. Janitors know everything. That day and night the big clock was five to seven minutes fast."

Jake thought for a moment. "Which would give W and Luke time to get downstairs for the balloons."

Tretheway nodded. "Remember Addie said no one we knew was missing at twelve?"

"That's right. But how. . ."

"Let me reconstruct." Tretheway drained his beer. "W and Luke took the other elevator up to the twelfth floor. Luke at the controls. They turned the lights out when they left and closed the door. Don't forget, Luke wasn't the brightest but he knew the ins and outs of the hotel. They went up to the Roof Garden. Easy enough for Luke to get a key. Mary came up in the first elevator, remember, and joined them on the roof. Luke locked the door again. Then we arrive. Go through our fire escape bit. Hear the scream."

"That was Mary Dearlove then?"

"I'd say so. Even though no one else heard it. But it was windy. Late at night. There must've been a confrontation of sorts. A scuffle. Then over she went."

"Gawd," Jake said. "Clutching the rabbit's foot."

"Yes. That was an oversight on W's part. But I imagine, in the excitement of the moment, smearing that stuff on her."

"Remember what Frank the barber told us? About what Luke said when they found Mary?"

"Ah. . .yes. Something about too many." Jake thought for a moment. "That's it. 'There's one too many'."

"That's the easy one. Too many gargoyles. That's how he spotted her. But he said something else."

"Can't recall."

"'She didn't do it'."

"Eh?"

"That's what he said."

"What's it mean? She didn't do what?"

"She didn't fly."

Jake stared at his boss without answering.

"Witches need a magical energy to fly. It comes from an ointment smeared thickly over their bodies. It usually contains potent herbs used in witchcraft. Monkshood, henbane, mandrake, hemlock. All mixed in a base of fat. Lard."

"The lard they found on Mary Dearlove?"

"Was not from the restaurant exhaust," Tretheway finished. "I'm also assuming it was regular lard. Not the traditional witches-of-old ointment. Do you know what their base was?"

Jake had a piece of cheese halfway to his mouth. He stopped.

"Fat from the bodies of boiled, unbaptized children."

Jake put the cheese back.

"Whether W believed it, or whether W did it to impress Luke, because he sure believed it, I don't know. Doesn't matter. Just another pushaway detail. Didn't change anything. They still threw her over. Then scampered back to the door. Unlocked it. Went down the stairs, locking the door behind them, to the waiting elevator, back to the ballroom in time to catch the balloons."

"By that time we were on the roof," Jake said.

"That's right," Tretheway said. "How's your beer?"

"I'm okay."

Tretheway took only one from the ice box. He came back to the easel and flipped the page over the back. "Know what's next?" he asked Jake.

"Squire Middleton."

"Not so fast." Tretheway wrote "Apr 13" on the clean sheet.

"Nothing happened then."

"Think about it."

"Surely you don't mean the five lawn bowls the cow swallowed?"

"No, no." Tretheway smiled. He wrote "The Great Barber Shop Robbery".

"That's part of it?" Jake asked.

"Witches use hair and fingernails from an intended victim to transmit a spell to that person."

"Then why don't we make a list. . ."

"Really, Jake. Jonathan (Jake) Small, Inspector Tretheway, Geoffrey Beezul, Zoë Plunkitt," Tretheway recited from memory. "Hell. Our whole office had its hair cut that day. And Frank thinks Garth Dingle and Gum were there too."

"You mean, one of those persons is the intended victim?"

"Yes."

"Well, for starters, you can rule out you and me."

"Why?"

"Surely you're not suggesting that you or I. . ."

"Jake." Tretheway held his hand up once more. "Keep an open mind."

Jake looked disturbed.

"Now W did this alone," Tretheway continued. "An early break-in. But W should've taken the money too. And maybe a couple of bay rum bottles. To make it look like an ordinary robbery. W made a mistake."

Tretheway turned back to the easel and wrote "Squire Middleton May 12." "The Squire," he said.

"Don't you mean the thirteenth?" Jake asked.

"I think not." Tretheway didn't explain further. "This was the most interesting murder to look into. I mean, professionally. It was the toughest to figure out. But once you did, it was the easiest. So simple."

"Oh?"

"Number one, the Squire wasn't murdered. Number two, his death hasn't a damn thing to do with W. Or our investigation."

Jake's eyes widened.

"Let me explain."

Jake leaned back.

"Squire Middleton was last seen alive shortly before eleven. The procedure is, at eleven o'clock, the conductor checks his car inside, turns off the lights, takes his bag, goes outside, shuts the door by hand, then goes around to the back, and using the rope, pulls the trolley off the live wire above the car and guides it under a hood on the roof. He lets the rope go and the pulley on the back of the car automatically takes up the slack. Simple. Takes five minutes. Then he goes home. The next day, the morning man reverses the procedure."

"I've seen them do it," Jake agreed.

"The Squire followed the regular routine. But when he pulled the trolley down, it jammed. So he let the rope go and climbed up the permanent ladder on the car's side to the roof. He put his bag down and examined the trolley. At the roof joint. Guess what he found?"

Jake shook his head.

"Two dead owls. At least two. Wedged under the trolley."

"Is that possible?" Jake asked.

"The boys at the car barn say so. Over the years they've found pigeons, rocks, even squirrels, jammed under the trolley. These were the first owls. That's why The Squire saved them. He dug them out, laid them down and pushed the trolley under the hood from his position on the roof. This was awkward. Took a little muscle. And you know, he wasn't in the best of shape."

Jake nodded.

"So there he was, finally, standing on the roof, puffing and panting, a dead owl in each hand, when he simply had a heart attack and died."

"Just like that," Jake said.

"Just like that."

"On the roof," Jake said.

Tretheway nodded. "Until the next day when the morning

man put the trolley back on the wire. No reason for him to go on the roof. He drove away. First sharp curve they hit at McKittrick bridge. . ."

"Where they found the bag."

Tretheway nodded. "The Squire's bag flew off. Second sharp curve?"

"King and James?" Jake guessed.

"Where the Squire flew off. Still dark. Very few people around. He lay there, in the shape of a pentacle squeezing the life out of two owls according to our innovative reports, until discovered. The street car long gone."

Tretheway put the pencil down and lit a cigar.

"I'll be damned," Jake said.

"Hm?" Tretheway puffed.

"It seems so simple the way you explain it. Even obvious."

"Have another beer." Tretheway went to the ice box again. He brought two quarts out with one hand.

"And W didn't lift a finger."

"No connection at all."

"I'll be damned."

"So now we can push it aside. It's not part of the picture." Tretheway laid his cigar across a squashed metal ash tray made from a WW1 artillery shell and picked up the pencil. "But I can't say the same for June."

He scribbled, "T. Warbucks, Jun 13, RFYYC."

"That was W," Jake said.

"'The venom'd plants wherewith she kills. . .'"

"Eh?"

"Something I read." Tretheway shook himself. "W. Yes. Definitely. I'm convinced W grew the Deadly Nightshade and made the poison from the black berries. Mixed it generously in one of Beezul's famous Banger milk bottles and marked it with a piece of string. Easy enough to do without getting caught if you were careful and knew the routine."

"But why Warbucks?"

"Mistake."

"Eh?"

Remember how Warbucks rushed into the locker after the race? Shouting for a Banger? He'd been dragged through the bay. Just a little on edge. Grabbed the closest bottle. W must've had a fit. Warbucks wasn't supposed to drink it. But after he downed the first half of the bottle, W had to just sit back and watch."

"Who was supposed to drink it?"

"Beezul."

"What?"

"Geoffrey Beezul."

Tretheway turned back to the easel. He exposed a fresh sheet and wrote, "Jul 13, Aug 13, Nothing." "Nothing happened in July or August because Beezul was up in Muskoka. You know how inaccessible his place is. And W doesn't have a timetable. W is in no hurry."

"How can you be sure?" Jake asked.

"Jake, I can't be. Nothing's sure. But he did get a haircut that day."

"We all did."

"Beezul was the only one to have a manicure as well." Tretheway held his hand in front of Jake, fingers outstretched. "Remember fingernails? Small point but they all add up. And he was certainly accessible at the Yacht Club. He was one of the few people who actually liked those foul-tasting Bangers. All W had to do was hand it to him."

"It's starting to sound plausible," Jake said. "But why Beezul?"

"I don't know." Tretheway pencilled the numbers "1692" on the pad. "But I'm sure it has something to do with the number we found on Hickory Island."

"You mean something happened in the year 1692?"

"I think so."

"What?"

"You tell me."

"Hm?"

"Research it."

"But how. . ."

"Jake. You're the Honours History grad. I'm sure you can handle it."

Jake looked embarrassed.

"Sept 13" Tretheway wrote on the pad, "P. Sprong. Fire." He turned to Jake. "This was pure W. With Luke now back on his feet filling his role as loyal evil assistant. It wasn't a mistake. W meant to kill Patricia Sprong."

"Why her?" Jake asked. "Why not go straight for Beezul?"

"W's saving him."

"For October."

"Yes. Now W has a timetable."

"The thirteenth."

"No, I don't think anything will happen on the thirteenth. But let's get back to your question. Why Patricia?" Tretheway lowered his voice.

"Let's climb into the brain of W. Let's look out at the world through those wide, misty translucent eyes and observe shadowy sisterhood. 'I am a witch,' W says, 'I can cast spells. I can fly backwards on my steed.'"

Jake shivered. Tretheway's voice returned to normal.

"How can W best serve Lucifer? Old Nick? The Prince of Darkness?" He wagged his pencil at Jake. "Kill Satan's enemies. Who better in W's warped mind than an active hardworking Captain in the Salvation Army? The original devil fighters. Remember her song? "I hate him and he hates me'?"

Jake nodded.

"Besides," Tretheway said half facetiously, "gives W something to do in September."

"Because, as you say, October is already planned."

"That's right."

"The big one."

"The finale."

"But. . ."

"Let's clean up the Sprong thing." Tretheway underlined the word 'Fire'. "Everybody knew Patricia took evening walks in Cootes'. W knows Cootes'. W, with Luke's help, grabbed her, probably tied her up, drugged her and waited in the woods for the witching hour. It was late and the weather was on their side. No one around. They carried her up the pile—difficult but not impossible—tied her to the stake, lit the fire and melted back into the woods."

"Gawd, that's cold-blooded!"

"Not for a witch."

"But how about Luke?"

"He seems to be falling more and more under W's spell. The loyal, unquestioning sidekick syndrome. He's no Rhodes Scholar, and don't forget, I'm sure they're both using some form of narcotic."

"I suppose."

"There's also a very good chance W would light the fire. Maybe even send Luke away first. Anyway, by the time the flames reached poor Patricia, W and Luke were well out of sight."

Jake sat quietly for a moment. "Maybe I'll have that beer now," Jake decided.

Tretheway took two more quarts out of the ice box. He handed one to Jake.

"Don't you have anything smaller?"

Tretheway didn't answer. Jake took the beer.

Tretheway flipped to a clean sheet on the pad. He wrote, 'October'. Underneath he printed a large '13'.

"Thirteenth? I thought you said. . ."

"New Year's Eve is probably the big holiday for Scots.

For Hebrews it's Hanukkah. For Christians, maybe Easter." Tretheway paused. "What's the biggie for witches?"

"Eh?"

"Think about it."

"Hallowe'en?"

Tretheway nodded. "The eve of All Saint's Day. No question." He pointed to the pad. "There's a tradition in the occult of doing things backwards. The Black Mass. The Lord's Prayer. Witches even ride their broomsticks backwards."

"So?" Jake said.

Tretheway circled the number 13. "Thirteen backwards," he scrawled '31', "is thirty-one. Last day of the month. Hallowe'en."

Tretheway took a long swig of beer. So did Jake. They stared at the scribblings on the pad.

"Now what do we do?" Jake asked.

"Stay alert," Tretheway said. "Keep an eye on Beezul. Especially on the thirty-first."

"Can we tell him?"

"I think not."

"What about Luke?"

"I don't want Luke. I want W."

"And W is?"

Tretheway shook his head. "I have to be sure."

Jake took a cracker and cheese.

"There's one more thing," Tretheway said.

Jake stopped chewing. "Hm?" He hated Tretheway's "one more things."

"We've had dashing to the ground and flying through the air. We've had poisoning. We've had burning at the stake. All legendary, murderous methods from the Kingdom of Darkness. There are others. But one stands out in my mind."

Jake waited.

"Water," Tretheway said.

"Not boiling babies again?"

"No, no. The water test."

"Oh?" Jake swallowed.

"In the dark days of old, persons accused of witchcraft were often thrown into a deep pond. If they sank and drowned, they were ruled innocent. If they floated and lived, they were found guilty and executed."

"A Hobson's choice."

"Exactly."

"So you think there'll be some sort of water thing on Hallowe'en?"

"Possible. This is in the smart guess category."

"Do you know where?"

"No. This is why we watch Beezul."

Jake finished off the crackers, drained his Blue and stood up. He could feel the beer. Fat Rollo thumped heavily as he jumped off the bed.

"So that's it then," Jake said.

"Till All Hallow's Eve," Tretheway said.

Fat Rollo waddled out of Tretheway's room. Jake concentrated on following the cat.

Chapter Twelve

October 13 approached quickly. Although Tretheway believed in his own prediction that nothing would happen, he took no chances. Through Addie, he arranged a euchre party. To avoid drawing attention to Beezul, Tretheway suggested two tables and gave a list of eight people to his sister including himself and Jake.

"You two aren't planning anything funny, are you?" Addie asked.

"No, no," Jake answered quickly.

"They're all going to wonder why through the week," Addie said. "On a Wednesday."

"Everything will be all right," Tretheway reassured.

"Just a party," Jake said.

Addie flounced off to the phone.

"She's a good kid," Tretheway said.

Jake smiled.

For the first round of the evening, Tretheway and Jake played opposite Bartholomew Gum and Zoë. The other table held the competent team of Cynthia Moon and Garth Dingle against Doc Nooner and the secret guest of honour, Beezul. Later on, the losers would rotate after rubbers. In the kitchen Addie chatted with Wan Ho, the ninth guest of her own choosing. As she often said, "An extra policeman never hurt anyone." The two casually served drinks, kibitzed with the players, replenished peanut dishes, substituted for anyone called to the bathroom and generally greased the social wheels of the party.

The evening went as Tretheway had forecast, except for the cards. He and Jake came second to Cynthia and Garth. Zoë and Gum were a close third, while Doc Nooner and Beezul were a distant last. There was a small scene near eleven o'clock when Beezul, after only one drink, stood up, fidgeted with his pants, and announced that he was tired and wanted to go home. Tretheway and Jake quickly pooh-poohed this.

"You can't go home now," Jake said. "You'll break up the tourney."

"Here. Have one for the other leg." Tretheway pushed a drink into his hand.

Beezul grumbled but played on.

The party broke up about twelve-thirty, which Tretheway felt was safe enough. He saw to it that everyone had a safe way home. Zoë drove Cynthia Moon, Gum was near enough to walk, Wan Ho rode with Doc Nooner and Garth had his own car.

Tretheway gave Jake an I-told-you-nothing-would-happen wink over Addie's shoulder before he closed the house up for the night.

It was close to the end of the month before Jake found out anything meaningful with his 1692 research, and he remained skeptical about all items except one.

"What have you got, Jake?" Tretheway and Jake sat, once again, in the privacy of Tretheway's quarters. It was the Thursday evening before Hallowe'en, which this year fell on a Sunday. Jake spread his notes out on Tretheway's desk and read them aloud.

"In 1692, Louis XIV of France attempted an invasion of England. The French fleet under Admiral de Tourville was defeated in a decisive engagement off 'La Hogue'—that's near Cherbourg —'and the invasion was turned back. After this victory, England remained mistress of the seas until almost our time'." Jake looked pleased with himself.

Tretheway shook his head.

"What's the matter?"

"What could that possibly have to do with our W?"

"But you said. . ."

"Do you have anything else?"

Jake reshuffled his notes. "'The Battle of Steinkirk. Victory of Luxembourg over William III'."

Tretheway shook his head again.

"How about Port Royal, Jamaica? 'Thousands killed in earthquake while tsunami obliterates private haven'."

"What's a tsunami?"

"A tidal wave."

"Then why didn't you say a tidal wave?"

Jake didn't say anything.

"I hope you're saving something."

"Well, there's one more. It's my favourite."

"Let's have it."

"The Salem witch trials."

"Ah." Tretheway's expression was the same as when he scratched his massive back against a door jamb.

"'1692, Salem Village.'" Jake read. "'Largest witch hunt in North America. Young girls met at the minister's house. Minister's slave, Tituba, filled their heads with tales of magic. Two of the girls lapsed into hysterical illness. Moaned, writhed on ground. Symptoms spread through child population of settlement. Thought to be bewitched. Finally girls accused others of witchcraft, including Tituba. Sir William Phipps appointed special commission of judges. Many more accusations. Village in grip of hysteria. Eventually two hundred arrested and nineteen executed'." Jake stopped reading. "Hard to believe. Nineteen people hanged."

"I think the total across the colony was twenty-four," Tretheway said.

"You know?"

"Jake. You can't research witchcraft without reading about Salem Village."

"Then why did I. . ."

"I had to know if anything else relevant happened that year. Someone had to come in through the back door." Tretheway pointed at Jake. "Through the year 1692. I came in through witchcraft. And we both met in Salem Village."

"But," Jake persisted, "how is that related exactly to our W?"

"Don't know. But it wouldn't hurt to make a few inquiries."

"Like what?"

"Sir William Phipps. I'd like to know the names of the judges he appointed. And the names of the ones they found guilty. We might get lucky."

"I should call Salem Village, I guess. Maybe the City Hall."

"I'd be inclined to call the local police. I'm sure they'll cooperate. This is business. Even though it may be unnecessary."

"Unnecessary?"

"There's only three days left till Hallowe'en. I doubt if we'd hear anything back before the thirty-first."

"So?"

"We might have the answers by then."

"Hm?"

"From W."

Chapter Thirteen

Everyone said that when Hallowe'en fell on a Sunday, fewer children went from door to door. Add to this bad weather, in the form of a thick bone-chilling fog and, they said, fewer still will show up. This didn't happen at the Tretheways' where Addie had the reputation of packing a toothsome Hallowe'en bag. She had spent the day baking miniature butter tarts. Wan Ho and Gum were in the kitchen inserting two tarts into each small bag, along with assorted candies and one chocolate BB bat. Zoë and Beezul shared the task of carrying them on a large tray to the front hall where Addie handed them out. Fat Rollo, looking like a fearsome ornament bought especially for the occasion, watched all the proceedings inside and out from the high hall window sill. Cynthia Moon had been invited but stayed home, she said, with a head cold. Doc Nooner was still at his office and Garth Dingle had to close up his pro shop, so neither was at Tretheways' to help. By seven-thirty they were about halfway through two hundred bags.

"I don't know about you," Tretheway said quietly to Jake, "but I've noticed more witches than anything else this year."

"You're right," Jake said. "Where are all the clowns? And funny faces?"

"Soldiers and tin men?"

"Knights of old? Princesses?"

Tretheway shook his head. "Sign of the times."

The hunchback dwarf appeared close to nine o'clock. Addie had the screen door open offering a tray to bigger boys who were probably trick-or-treating for the last time. An impish creature suddenly pushed the boys roughly aside and grabbed several bags from the tray, almost knocking it from Addie's hands. A low growl came from its hideous, upturned mask. Addie screamed. The dwarf turned and ran awkwardly, as though crippled, down the sidewalk. Its long black cloak, misshapen by the huge hunch, swept across the wet grass. The older boys dropped their bags and ran the other way. Jake got there just in time to see the dwarf disappear into the fog.

"You okay?" Jake asked.

"Yes, yes." Addie had recovered. "Gave me such a start."

"What was it?"

"It looked like a gnome. A very ugly, rude, garden gnome."

"What the hell's going on?" Tretheway appeared on the porch.

"Everything's okay," Jake said. "A kid scared Addie. Dressed up as a dwarf. Hunchback and everything."

"He growled," Addie said. "And he looked awful. He had this horrible mask. Fuzzy hair. And a long cloak."

"You're supposed to look awful on Hallowe'en," Tretheway said. "It would be unusual if he had on a three-piece business suit."

"That's not funny."

Tretheway didn't answer.

"And he didn't say thank you either." Addie went back into the kitchen for the last few bags.

By nine-thirty all was quiet. At ten, Zoë Plunkitt left for home, dropping Gum on her way. Tretheway and Jake sat at the kitchen table sampling Addie's butter tarts.

"How many of those have you had?" she asked her brother.

"Two," Tretheway answered. Jake had counted eleven

but, he thought, they were quite small. Addie disappeared with her goodies into the common room where Wan Ho and Beezul were chatting with several student boarders.

"I had to tell Wan Ho," Tretheway said.

"That's good," Jake said.

"Not the whole story. Just enough so he'll keep an eye on Beezul. And be ready to help if he's needed."

"I feel better."

"With two squad cars."

"Eh?"

"At Central. Waiting for his call."

"Maybe you'd better tell me the whole plan," Jake said.

"Simplicity itself," Tretheway answered. "We follow Beezul tonight."

"We?"

"You and me."

"I thought maybe Wan Ho would come along."

"No. I want him here. To watch the house. And to call in the police officially."

"That's why we're using the Pontiac?"

"Right. Remember I asked you to double-check the car. I'd hate to have anything go wrong."

"Not to worry. Full of gas." Jake reassured. "And I tuned it up myself."

Tretheway nodded. "Okay. We follow Beezul to his house. Wait maybe five minutes. Then you run down the block. There's a pay phone. Make sure you have change. Call Wan Ho."

Jake wondered to himself why he always had to do the leg work.

"He'll send the cars in. They'll wait with us. Until W comes."

"Is W going to do the deed there?"

"Probably not." Tretheway paused. "Although there's a

couple of swimming pools in that neighbourhood. And there's a dammed-up creek just under the mountain. But it's not too practical. Not too private. No." Tretheway tossed another butter tart into his mouth. "They intend to kidnap Beezul. Take him somewhere. But it doesn't matter. By that time we'll have W."

"You're not going to wait and see?"

"No point. Too dangerous, for one thing. W will be there. With all the paraphernalia. Caught red-handed. With Luke. Hard for W to explain. Break in. Abduction. I'm sure W will break down when confronted. Simple as that."

"I hope so."

"What could go wrong?"

Jake shrugged.

"Certainly not your car."

Jake didn't answer.

At quarter after ten, Beezul announced he was going home. Tretheway didn't protest.

"Be careful, Geoffrey," Addie warned. "It's still foggy."

"Stick to the main streets," Tretheway suggested.

"Don't worry." Beezul put his coat on. "Straight to Main Street, then right on Dundurn. And just about follow it home."

Tretheway and Jake exchanged smiles.

The minute Beezul went out the door, Tretheway and Jake grabbed their coats from the front closet. Jake ran down the hall and out the back door.

"Where's he going?" Addie asked.

"To start the car," Tretheway said.

"At this hour?"

"It's not late, Addie," Wan Ho said.

"Something funny's going on."

"Addie," Tretheway explained, "We're just looking after Beezul. Wan Ho will stay here till we get back. There's nothing funny going on."

"Then why did Jake borrow a nickel from me?"

Tretheway shook his head and went out the front door.

They followed as close as they dared behind Beezul's sedan. If anything, the fog was thicker. Jake had the wipers on and the inadequate defroster set at full. The leather seats were cold to the touch.

"Great night for Hallowe'en." Jake peered through a small area of clear windshield.

"Not the best." Tretheway's cigar didn't help the visibility problem.

Jake turned carefully onto Main Street well behind Beezul. There were no other cars in sight.

"Good of him to give us directions," Jake commented.

"That was a break," Tretheway said.

"Is this close enough?"

"Just about right".

It took them about ten minutes to reach the Dundurn intersection where Beezul said he would turn right. Beezul swerved suddenly and turned left.

"Hey!" Jake shouted. Beezul sped up. "He's turned the wrong way."

"Damn!" Tretheway cursed.

Jake jerked the Pontiac left in pursuit. The straight eight engine had little trouble in reaching their spot again, a discreet distance behind the sedan.

"What's going on?" Jake asked.

"I don't know," Tretheway said, "but I don't like it."

A huge tractor trailer came toward them out of the fog. The blazing lights of the rig almost blinded them as it rumbled by.

Jake squinted through the windshield, now mostly clear. "Did you see that?" he said.

"What?"

"No! It couldn't be!"

"Couldn't be what?"

"Another head. A passenger. When those truck lights went by. I thought I saw someone else in Beezul's car."

"Impossible." Now Tretheway did his best to lean forward and peer through the windshield. "Wait for another car."

"Here comes one."

The two strained their eyes into the fog. Beezul was clearly illuminated against the oncoming headlights. The car passed by quickly.

"See anything," Jake asked.

"No."

"Must've been my imagination."

"I hope so," Tretheway said, "although it would explain Beezul's behaviour."

"You mean someone..."

"C'mon," Tretheway said. "We're falling behind."

They followed Beezul along the four-lane thoroughfare that led out of Fort York. Once past the city limits, fewer homes appeared, most with no lights. And only an occasional car passed them going in the opposite direction. The road became two tortuous hilly lanes.

"Where are we?" Tretheway asked.

"King's Highway Two. Heading east."

"This isn't working out. Something has to happen before twelve."

"He's gone!" Jake shouted.

"What?" Tretheway leaned dangerously close to the windshield.

"He must've turned off."

"Slow down."

Jake hit the brakes at the concealed intersection. Tretheway saw tail lights out of his side window.

"There he is!" Tretheway shouted. "Turn right."

Jake reacted immediately but the long-nosed Pontiac roadster was never considered nimble. He made a much wider turn than anticipated, crossed a corner of someone's front lawn and splashed through a gigantic puddle on the left side of the road. A wall of water hit the windshield. Enough came through the convertible top joint to put out Tretheway's cigar. The car sputtered to a stop.

"Why did you stop?" Tretheway shouted.

"I didn't stop. The car stopped."

Jake pushed the starter button. The starting engine whined but the motor stubbornly refused to turn over.

"Make it go!" Tretheway shouted.

"It's flooded."

"So much for your tune-up."

Jake didn't wait to explain. He jumped out of the driver's seat into the ankle-deep water. Splashing his way to the rumble seat for dry rags, then back to the front of the car, he wrenched open one side of the engine cover and frantically tried to dry the hot, perspiring engine and wires. Tretheway watched helplessly as the red lights of Beezul's car grew fainter.

"He's going!" Tretheway shouted.

Jake fastened the engine cover and jumped back in the car. He floored the accelerator and turned the key.

"He's gone," Tretheway shouted.

Jake closed his eyes and took a few precious seconds to pray silently to whichever patron saint guided the fortunes of first-class constables. He pressed the starter button. A muffled explosion blew the exhaust system, but the car lurched into life.

"What was that?" Tretheway said.

"Backfire."

"What's the noise?"

"Blew the muffler." Jake smiled at his boss. "But it's going."

Tretheway shook his head. "Let's go."

They bored noisily into the fog in the direction Beezul's

143

tail lights had gone. There were no decisions to be made because there was only one road—until the intersection.

"What now?" Jake idled the rumbling engine.

"What's ahead?" Tretheway asked.

"Dead end."

"And right?"

"Back to Fort York."

Tretheway pointed left and looked a question.

"Spotty residential, small farms. Golf Club. Then the Village of Wellington Square. And eventually, Toronto."

"That's it."

"Toronto?"

"No. The Golf Club."

"My Golf Club?"

"Think about it." Tretheway struck the fingers of his substantial left hand one at a time to list his points. "Has to be nearby. Time is pressing. Eighteen holes all neatly numbered. Right?"

"What's that mean?"

Tretheway ignored Jake's question. "Private. No one around. And I'll bet there's water on the course. A small pond maybe."

"Yes, there is."

"Let's go." Tretheway pointed left.

Because of the fog, heavier by the bay, it took them fifteen minutes to reach the WSGCC; normally it would've taken five. They pulled into the empty parking lot. Jake switched off the full-throated engine. Tretheway rolled down his window and listened. Moisture from the trees dripped onto the fabric of Jake's car. Every few moments the sonorous bleat of a fog horn swept across the distant wartime shipping lanes. Night lights from the nearby pro shop were barely discernible; the clubhouse across the road appeared only as a dim shadow.

"Great night for a murder," Jake said.

"What's the time?" Tretheway asked.

"Eleven-thirty."

Tretheway opened the door.

"Where are you going?" Jake asked.

"We can't sneak up on anyone in this tractor."

Jake ignored his boss's remark. "I've been thinking. Why couldn't we borrow Garth's cart?"

"What?"

"Garth Dingle has a golf cart. Made it himself. For driving around the course."

"Is it quiet?"

"Electric."

"Where is it?"

"At his house." Jake anticipated the next question. "This time of year, he lives on the course."

"Let's get it." Tretheway slammed the door.

The car broke the night's silence again as Jake maneuvered the Pontiac across the parking lot to where the service road started. They followed the narrow dirt track around the perimeter of the golf course to the Pro's summer home. Garth stood on the verandah.

"I came out to see the four-engined bomber," he said as soon as Jake shut off the engine.

"Muffler blew," Jake said.

"We need your car," Tretheway said without preamble.

"Now?" Garth smiled. "You taking up golf, Inspector?"

Tretheway explained what was going on as much as he could, as quickly as he could, with Jake filling in the odd detail.

Garth understood the urgency.

"The cart's plugged in around back."

They went around the house at a fast walk.

"I hope there's enough juice." Garth pulled the cart's plug from the wall and coiled up the wire.

"What do you mean?" Tretheway asked.

"I usually charge the batteries overnight."

"Can we all fit in?" Jake asked.

Garth checked himself before he automatically answered yes. He eyed Tretheway who was towering over the cart: big uncovered head, huge shoulders supporting the tent-like rubber slicker hanging only inches above his king-size boots.

"Jake," Garth said. "You have to walk."

"I should have known," Jake said to himself.

Garth turned the key as Tretheway climbed into the passenger side. The two big men fitted snugly into the ample bench seat. Tretheway lurched backwards as Garth floored the go pedal and the cart—without enough warning, Tretheway thought—sped down the driveway. Garth jammed on the brakes. Jake almost ran into them.

"What's the matter? Tretheway asked.

"Where are we going?" Garth asked.

"Isn't it obvious?"

"Not to me."

Tretheway twisted around as much as he could. "Jake?" Jake looked blank.

"Think numbers. One, three, thirteen."

"Ah," Jake said. "The thirteenth hole."

"That's this way then," Garth said.

The cart took off left, surprisingly fast, with Jake padding after. Garth drove the golf cart as though he enjoyed it. He steered over long rough and cut fairway with equal ease, between sand traps, up and down the slight hillocks that protected the bunkers and occasionally bumped over tree roots or a small ditch. Tretheway hung on to the dashboard with one hand. The other shone his flashlight ineffectually into the chill fog. Garth's electric machine whined almost silently while the fat oversized tires, punching down on the soft wet undergrowth, made no more noise than a light breeze.

"We should slow down before we get there," Tretheway suggested in spasmodic jerks that matched the action of the bouncing vehicle.

Garth pushed the brake pedal down. The cart skewed to a stop. "We're here."

"Eh?"

"The thirteenth. We're right beside the green." Garth pointed toward the flag.

Tretheway grunted himself out of the cart. His eyes swept from the green back towards the tee as far as the fog would allow.

"Where is it?" he said.

"Where's what?"

"The water. The pond."

"There isn't any."

"Damn!"

They both turned at the sound of Jake's approaching footsteps. With the breath he had left, all he could do was wave.

"You're sure this is the thirteenth?" Tretheway said.

Jake nodded.

"Certainly," Garth said.

Tretheway spun around and stepped toward the flagstick. Garth bit his tongue as he watched the deep depressions the big policeman's heels made in the soft green. Tretheway lifted the limp wet flag away from the stick. He shook it a few times, then stretched it out.

"Then what the hell's this?"

Garth and Jake crossed the green carefully until they were close enough to make out the numbers one and eight: eighteen.

"I don't understand," Garth said.

"Me neither," Jake said.

"Is there water on the eighteenth?"

"Yes, there is," Garth said.

147

"A big holding pond," Jake said.

"The bugger's switched flags."

Tretheway turned and ran for the cart. Garth and Jake looked at each other, then chased after Tretheway. Jake jumped back this time and no one objected. The cart leaped forward. They retraced their path past Garth's house, creating their own miniature tunnel in the fog. Tretheway hung on with both hands and Jake hugged the bag racks as Garth twisted and turned the cart, following short cuts known only to him. He sped across the parking lot and stopped at the main road.

"Why are we stopping?" Tretheway asked.

"The highway." Garth looked left and right. "We have to go along a bit. The eighteenth's on the other side." He pointed the flashlight in Tretheway's lap. "You're the headlight."

Tretheway let go of the dash and picked up the light. Garth pushed the go pedal to the floor and turned onto the highway, while Tretheway waved the flashlight in front of him. Jake looked nervously behind. He wondered how he could explain an accident to Addie or anyone: two FY policeman and a golf pro, close to midnight, in an unlicensed vehicle on the King's Highway in a heavy fog. Fortunately, no cars came from either direction. They turned off a few hundred yards down the road.

"Almost there," Garth said.

The cart was humming up the next rise when it gave out.

"That's it," Garth said.

"What's the matter?"

"Out of juice." Garth put his finger to his lips, "But the pond's just over the hill," he whispered.

They left the cart quietly and climbed up the last incline. Jake rubbed the circulation back into his hands and arms. He noticed that Garth was carrying the golf club.

"Where'd you get that?"

"Always keep one in the cart." He hefted the five iron with one big hand and smacked the blade into the other palm. "The old equalizer. Where's yours?"

"I don't have one," Jake said.

"Where's your revolver?" Tretheway asked.

"You never said..."

"Damn! Do I have to tell you everything?"

"Where's yours?"

"Listen," Garth said.

The trio stopped. They heard the drone of an aircraft high above the weather. A car engine laboured, the fog horn persisted, a lake freighter answered, but all sounds were distant. Then they heard what Garth heard.

"There " he said.

"What's that?"

"A voice."

"Man or woman?"

"Don't know."

"Singing?"

"More like a chant." They bent over double and scampered to the top of the hill. Flopping full-length on the wet grass, the adventurous three slowly, ever so slowly, raised their heads above the rim of the hill. They peered down through the long wild grass that bordered the natural amphitheatre of the eighteenth fairway. A scene that evoked a perfectly cast-and-staged outdoor Shakespearean production played itself out before them. The mood lighting was flawless, the scenery impossible to improve and the costumes in perfect character. But this was real; no play acting.

The optical centre of the tableau was light. In a bowl— bronze, Tretheway thought— fire crackled, adding sparks and fumes to an already saturated atmosphere. The flames were reflected dully in the pond behind. Two figures danced and cavorted haphazardly around the blaze, sometimes brilliantly lit, sometimes thrust into silhouette. The larger figure looked like a Hallowe'en witch: long, ample cloak, pointed hat, now bent, with a floppy brim, all black, with white spiky hair atop a blood-red scowling mask.

"W," Tretheway whispered. "At last, we meet W."

The smaller one bounced ungracefully around the circle in similar garb, but there was no hat on its black frizzly hair.

"Addie's ugly garden gnome." Jake grabbed Tretheway's arm. "That's who I saw in the car."

"Keep it down," Tretheway said.

"Let's get 'em" Garth waved his five iron.

"Hold on," Tretheway said. "Where's Beezul?"

The chanting started again, low to begin with, then becoming louder as the two continued their mad dance around the burning bowl. W leaned dangerously close to the fire more than once, as though inhaling the fumes, once lifting the gnome so he too could enjoy its vapours. Loud cackling laughter mingled with the incantations.

"They're high as kites," Garth said.

"What do you suppose is in the fire?" Jake asked.

"Henbane, I'll wager," Tretheway said.

Odd words and disjointed phrases whirled through the fog in frightful voices neither Tretheway, Jake or Garth recognized.

"Emperor Lucifer...beyond the river Styx...Master of rebellious spirits...I deny my baptism...deny the creator of Heaven and earth..."

W and the gnome reversed their direction around the fire. Their tempo intensified.

"Welcome all bogarts...goblins, foul-smelling apes...blood-sucking imps...servants of Satan...when bitches howl...warm blood is spilled..."

They shouted now, almost in unison. The three observers heard every word.

"I cleave to thee, Prince of Darkness. In thee I believe."

"Gawd." Jake's skin crawled.

"When do we charge?" Garth asked.

"When we're told." Tretheway said.

Activity at the fire stopped abruptly. An eerie silence followed. It seemed interminable. Tretheway could hear Jake and Garth breathing. For a wild moment he thought they had been discovered. Even the fog horn was silent. Then W broke the silence.

"Time to seek retribution." W ran to the side. "For the evil that was done to my family." The gnome gambolled after. They picked up something large and light-colored and carried it back to the fire, holding it so its head came close to the fumes. In the light, Tretheway could make out arms and legs.

"Christ! It's Beezul."

"He's buck naked," Garth said.

"Why's he all doubled up?" Jake said.

"Fill your head with hog's bean," W shouted. "Inhale the baleful flowerspray. Ingest the heady roasting seeds till limbs lose their certainty. Then enter the witches' cauldron of madness." They passed Beezul's head through the smoke several times. "Enough!" W shrieked.

W and the gnome carried their bundle down the slight incline toward the pond. At the water's edge, they swung Beezul back and forth between them.

" I commit thee, evil progeny of Horatio Beezul, to Satan's deep!" W shrieked rhythmically in time to the swings. On the word "deep", they released Beezul. He flew into the pond.

"Now!" Tretheway shouted.

He led the charge down the slope. Garth ran close behind shaking his five iron in the air. Jake followed. All, on the verge of losing control, were screaming. W and the gnome froze in their tracks and gaped at the onrushing trio. Halfway down, Tretheway's feet slid out from under him. He tobogganed, spinning on his rubber slicker the rest of the way. Missing the burning tripod by inches, he wiped out most of the circles and pentacles scratched earlier by W in the sand trap and picked off the gnome as neatly as a bowling ball drops the solitary pin in a successful spare. They both skipped into the pond like flat stones.

When Jake got there, Tretheway and the gnome were wildly thrashing in the centre of the pond, but there was no sign of Beezul.

"The rope!" Tretheway splashed. "Pull the rope!"

Jake looked around frantically. He made out a thick, taut rope emerging from the water. It was attached to a nearby tree trunk. He started pulling.

Garth grabbed the witch, but quickly realized that W was too far out of it to go anywhere. He ran to help Jake. The two pulled Beezul, coughing and sputtering, out of the cold pond.

When Tretheway reached the shore, he hurled the gnome onto the grass. Luke had lost his mask and cloak in pond. He rose from a squatting position to his regular height and scampered over to W where he groped to take her hand. Tretheway went to help Beezul.

Jake was trying to untie the main rope around Beezul's waist. Garth fumbled with the smaller knots of twine. Beezul's arms were crossed, his thumbs tied to the opposite toes.

"Classic," Tretheway observed.

"He's coming around," Jake said.

They stood him up and pummelled some life back into his shivering body. Garth stripped his own heavy sweater off and pulled it over Beezul's shoulders. It barely covered his privates.

"You okay?" Holding Beezul's head steady between his

huge hands, Tretheway stared into pupils much larger than normal.

"Must've fallen overboard, Skipper." Beezul tried to hitch his pants up.

"What's his trouble?" Garth asked.

"He'll be all right." He angled his head towards the flames in the bronze bowl. "Too much henbane."

They approached the fire. Luke was clutching W's hand and arm, with his face buried in the deep folds of the witch's cloak. A muffled chant came from W. Tretheway slowly reached out and removed W's hat. Gently he lifted the mask from W's face.

"I break away from earth. Soar across the midnight sky. Above the lights. Above the trees. Across the yellow moon. I buss the clouds. In my nighttime steed. My besom. My distaff."

Without a mask W's words were dreamy but clear. The heavy black makeup that ringed her wide black eyes ran with moisture. Her beet-red lip colouring mixed greasily into the thick witch's pomade which was smeared un-evenly over her face and into her dishevelled hair.

"Zoë," Tretheway said quietly.

"Anywhere. Anytime. In the twinkling of a bat's eye. A flick of a hare's tail."

"Zoë," Tretheway repeated.

"Boss." Jake put his hand on Tretheway's arm. "She can't hear you."

"She's on funny street," Garth said.

Then Zoë Plunkitt began to laugh: a low witch's laugh, a private, disturbing, primeval cackle.

Tretheway walked away and threw W's mask and hat into the darkness. He turned and eyed the fire. It still burned brightly. He took a few quick, calculated steps toward it. Swinging his overweight but muscular leg, Tretheway caught the blazing bowl squarely on its bottom, sending it in a graceful arc over the heads of his startled friends: spewing sparks and evil, flaming seeds into the fog, it splashed into the pond. It hissed noisily before it sank. There were no other sounds.

"Let's find the cars," Tretheway said. "And get the hell out of here."

Epilogue

In early November, Allied troops captured San Salvo on their way to Rome; the Americans landed in the Solomons; Russians took the City of Kiev and an RCN destroyer was badly damaged off the coast of Spain.

On the home front, old-age pensions were raised from twenty-three to twenty-eight dollars a month. With this extra money, the seniors of Fort York could buy leather windbreakers for $11.95, a full-length ladies' muskrat coat for $244 or used cars— overhauled and refinished —for as little as $75.

"The FY Tagger Football Club plays Navy tomorrow"; "Maple Leafs tied Detroit Red Wings yesterday", and "Irving Berlin's *This is the Army*, starring men of the armed forces, including Lt. Ronald Reagan, flicked across the silver screen".

All these important and not-so-important items appeared in the *FY Expositor*, Friday, November 5th.

"Guy Fawke's Day, Addie." Jake was reading the paper.

"Today?" Addie asked. "That's right. 'Please to remember, the fifth of November'..."

"'Gunpowder, treason and plot'," Tretheway finished, waking from his light evening doze in the parlour.

"At least we won't have to worry about the thirteenth this month," Jake said.

"That's right." Addie lowered her section of the paper.

"I can't get Zoë Plunkitt out of my mind. And why she did, you know, what she did."

"Revenge," Tretheway said.

"Addie." Tretheway straightened up in his easy chair. "Look at the facts. 1692. Salem Village. Horatio Increase Beezul, a direct ancestor of our Geoffrey was appointed Judge. During the witch scare. He sentenced one Phadrea Plunkitt, a direct ancestor of Zoë, to the water test. She drowned. Zoë stumbled across this on one of her many trips to New England."

"I thought she went to a place called Danvers," Addie said.

"She did, Addie," Jake explained. "Salem Village was just outside the city of Salem. After the trials and the great recantation, the elders changed the name of the village to — guess what?"

Addie stared at Jake.

"Danvers," Jake said. "It's called that today."

Addie's lips formed a silent oh.

"Remember she took Luke there once," Tretheway said. "For some sort of meeting."

"Sabbat," Jake said.

"Well anyway, with a bunch of witches."

"Coven," Jake said.

"You want to tell the story?"

Jake shook his head.

"What'll happen to her now?" Addie interrupted. "And Luke."

"There's no doubt about their guilt," Tretheway said. "But I doubt either will hang."

Addie frowned.

"They'll put Zoë away." Jake looked at Addie. "Like in a hospital. And probably the same thing for Luke."

"With bars on the window," Tretheway said.

"Tell me," Addie asked, "how did he get Beezul to drive him to the golf club?"

"Threatened him," Tretheway said. "Must've scared the life out of Beezul popping up in the back seat like that. Remember when his car swerved at Dundurn?"

Jake nodded.

"I'm glad Geoffrey's all right," Addie said.

"He's remarkably fit after all he went through," Jake agreed.

"The henbane helped," Tretheway said.

"That's right," Jake said. "Doesn't remember much. Said he had a headache for days."

"But let's go back to Zoë Plunkitt," Tretheway continued. "After she found out about her wronged ancestor and Judge Horatio Beezul, she started spying on Geoffrey. And how better to do that than work with him? Or sail for him. Then she carefully made her plans. And we all know where that led."

"But what I still don't understand," Addie persisted, "is why she went to all that trouble? The Hickory Island thing. The rabbit. The belladonna. The bonfire. Why did she pretend to be a witch?"

No one said anything for about thirty seconds.

"Addie," Jake said, "wild as it might seem, Zoë believed that she *was* a witch."

Another short silence punctuated the conversation.

"I'll go you one better," Tretheway said. "Zoë Plunkitt *is* a witch."

The fire crackled. Fat Rollo sighed in his dream and blew a small whirlwind of ashes across the hearth. Addie folded up her newspaper and stood up. "Bedtime for me." She left the parlour.

Tretheway went back to his paper. Jake left his seat to fiddle with the radio. After ten minutes of trying to get the eleven o'clock war news from London and receiving nothing but shrill whistles and static on the short wave band, he gave up and switched it off.

"Bad night" he said. "Guess I'll hit the sack."

"Good night, Jake," Tretheway said.

Jake opened the sliding doors and stopped. He looked back at his boss. "This witchcraft business," he started.

"Hm?" Tretheway put down his paper.

"You don't really believe Zoë Plunkitt's a witch?" Jake paused. Tretheway's expression didn't change. "I mean, everything that they say — about casting spells, brewing up a storm, withering crops, making milk sour, turning into animals, flying across the sky. That's all Wizard of Oz kid stuff. Old wives' tales. B movie scripts. Right?"

A hint of a smile crossed Tretheway's face. "Jake. You, Jonathan Small, B.A., man of letters, honours grad. You're asking me? A simple traffic policeman. About the secrets of the mystic universe? Really."

"Yeh. I know." Jake looked sheepish. "It was a dumb question."

"There's nothing to worry about." Tretheway smiled. "We'll all sleep tight."

"I know."

"But I don't step on any spiders."

Jake's frown returned as he slid the doors shut.

Tretheway grinned broadly. He leaned back in his big chair and quietly blew smoke rings for a while. Finally he pushed himself up and tossed the wet cigar butt into the dying fire. He nudged the cat's stomach with his foot. Fat Rollo opened one eye and hissed.

Tretheway drank a quick quart of ale while making his rounds on the ground floor. He left the empty beside the ice box on his way upstairs. Just before climbing into bed he automatically checked his desk clock. Both hands pointed at twelve. He pulled the blind up on his tall bedroom window and opened the sash. The bracing November air whisked into the room. Tretheway looked into the night. Enough leaves still clung to the hard maple trees to rustle pleasantly but not enough to obscure the pale yellow orb of a full moon. An owl hooted distinctly three times.